I0545208

A Sycamore Secret

STACEY WEEKS

Copyright © 2023 by Stacey Weeks

All rights reserved.

Scripture quotations are from The Holy Bible, English Standard
Version® (ESV®), copyright © 2001 by Crossway, a publishing ministry
of Good News Publishers. Used by permission. All rights reserved.

No part of this book may be reproduced in any form or by any
electronic or mechanical means, including information storage and
retrieval systems, without written permission from the author, except
for the use of brief quotations in a book review.

ISBN: 978-1-7387413-5-9

Grace and Love Publishing

Free Short Story

Download at StaceyWeeks.com

When sweet peppers and jalapeño mix,
anything can happen.

Addison avoids visiting the city. He hates the crowds, traffic, and pace. He especially hates the compact vehicle the rental company insists he'd reserved. But then he runs into Sarah. Or, more accurately, she runs into him, mixing sweet peppers and jalapeño with burnt metal, petrol, hot pavement, and her desperation to not merely survive life in the city but find a place to thrive. Addison isn't looking for a weekend thrill or a romantic entanglement anymore than she is. They both want to go home. Maybe, together, they'll find their way.

Praise for The Sycamore Standoff

Weeks is a writer I count on for sweet contemporary romances with faith messages to make me think. Sycamore Standoff combines sympathetic characters with heartening takeaways about the freedom of living in grace and the power of community.

— AUTHOR EMILY CONRAD

The town of Sycamore Hill is warm and welcoming. The heart of God shines throughout the story. I really enjoyed The Sycamore Stand Off.

— JULIA - BOOK REVIEWER,
CHRISTIAN BOOKAHOLIC

One of the things I enjoy about Stacey Weeks' writing is her ability to present a powerful & touching gospel message organic to the story, without it feeling forced or preachy. Instead of stopping an entertaining story for a sermon, Weeks uses the faith-centered elements to enhance the characters' journeys on the page and point to the Source of peace, strength, and courage.

— CARRIE ~ BOOK REVIEWER, READING IS MY SUPERPOWER

More Fiction by Stacey Weeks

SYCAMORE HILL

To Sweet Beginnings in Sycamore Hill

The Sycamore Standoff

His Sycamore Sweetheart

The Sycamore Slopes

One Sycamore Sunday

A Sycamore Secret

MISTLETOE MEADOWS

Mistletoe Melody

Mistletoe Mission

Mistletoe Movie Star

STAND ALONE TITLES

Fatal Homecoming

The Builder's Reluctant Bride

In Too Deep

To God, who has done far more for me than I could ask for or imagine.

So, whether you eat or drink, or whatever you do,
do all to the glory of God.

1 Corinthians 10:31

Chapter One

Some days, she had to confess the spotlight had lost its brilliance. Internet sensation Kathryn Withers mugged another smile in front of her boyfriend's bakery. "Did you get that?" She broke character, but she didn't move from where she stood in case Gloria hadn't captured the clip.

"I think so." Gloria scrunched her face and peered at the camera's digital screen. "Want to see?" She held out the device.

Releasing her sucked-in gut, Kathryn took the camera and reversed the footage. "I love the way you caught the sun glinting off the gilded sign for *The Muffin Man* and still managed to angle the shot so there's no glare on the front display window. And you kept me front and centre." Heat burned Kathryn's cheeks. She sounded vain. "You're really good at this. Ethan's going to love it."

Every so often, Kathryn gave her boyfriend's shop a shout-out on her show. A little free PR came with the territory of dating an influencer. Ethan was adding a coffee roasting lab to his bakery to set himself apart from the seemingly endless coffee chains opening store fronts in and around Sycamore Hill. The other businesses might have big bucks behind their brand, but *The Muffin Man* was the only artisan shop that roasted fresh beans onsite.

"I'll add it to my list of skills," Gloria quipped. "If the daycare reduces my hours anymore, I might need a side hustle."

"I'd offer you a job in a heartbeat. A volunteer job, of course." Kathryn gave her a sheepish grin. "Because internet TV doesn't pay beans, not even coffee beans."

Gloria tipped her head toward the bakery. "Wanna go inside? I'm starving."

"Absolutely. My treat." Buying her friend a cup of the best coffee blend in town was the least she could do, and considering she was heading into an evening of editing, coffee was practically a necessity.

Keeping her web show, *Sycamore Hill at Sunrise*, running required long hours and a heart devoted to the craft. It was the cost of fame, and being admired was all Kathryn ever wanted. However, after years producing the show, the thrill had lessened. Not that she'd admit that to anyone. To the rest of the world, she was Kathryn Withers, cookbook author, internet sensation, and social media influencer. But inside, she would always be Kathy, a little girl, looking for a place to fit in.

Gloria's phone chimed. Glancing at the screen, she said, "Meg's working today. She says she has news for us." With thumbs typing faster on the keypad than some people managed on a computer, Gloria replied to their friend's text message.

"Another good reason to call it a wrap. We can grab a coffee inside and hear her news." They had more than enough footage. Kathryn tended to over-record and then ruthlessly cut. She meticulously produced each minute of her show. That was the only way to ensure she delivered what her audience expected: a little self-deprecating humor, a pretty face, and up-to-date local news. Some called it gossip, but Kathryn disagreed. Gossip had a cruel bent, and what Kathryn did was harmless. She could never be unkind, having been on the receiving end of gossip too many times.

"Are you coming to the church potluck on Sunday?"

"Depends. Are you making sushi?"

An unladylike snort exploded from Gloria. "I learned my lesson. I'm sticking to noodles, cheese, and some sort of creamy condensed soup." Enough time had passed since Gloria's sushi disaster that she could laugh about it.

Kathryn admired her friend. Coming home to Sycamore Hill hadn't been easy, and finding her place in the community as Pastor Owen's bride had been even harder. But she'd persevered, and now she and Owen were happily married, and those troubles were a distant memory.

Kathryn folded her arms across her stomach. Was there a happily ever after for her? Her attention moved to the film equipment that needed packing. She loaded up the bag. Sure, she'd achieved what she'd always thought she wanted—the spotlight, admiration, and success. But she never expected it to be so exhausting or unfulfilling. It came with a lurking loneliness. A yearning that never felt fulfilled. From the outside, she looked like she had it all, but it was an illusion. One she was just as desperate to maintain as she was to shake free from its grasp.

Kathryn slung the packed camera bag over her shoulder and followed Gloria through the bakery door. A string of bells announced their arrival.

Meg looked up from behind the cash register. "Grab a table. I'll bring you coffees in a minute." She handed a customer his change.

Kathryn wove through the tiny tables for two and four people, choosing one with a clear line of sight into the kitchen. Ethan pulled a tray of muffins from the large industrial-sized oven. A hairnet tamed his dark mop. Kathryn loved the subtle wave in his hair and how he kept it just long enough that she could thread her fingers through it at the nape. Most customers came for the menu, but Kathryn came for her Muffin Man, who, incidentally, was rocking the apron she'd given him last Christmas. She'd silk-screened the question *Do you know the Muffin Man?* on the front of it. At first, she'd worried the apron had been a mistake since Ethan's dad used to tease him by dancing around him and singing that song. When Ethan had read the caption, she explained that the song needed new memories attached to it. And after only the tiniest hesitation, he'd pulled it over his head and whirled around, modelling it. He'd worn it every day since.

And her heart did somersaults every time.

Ethan's dad also called him Betty Crocker, but Kathryn hadn't yet come up with a clever gift idea to redeem that slight.

Meg clunked two mugs onto the table and poured coffee from the pot she carried in her other hand. "This is Ethan's latest blend. You'll appreciate its notes of vanilla and creamy body."

"Kathryn's appreciating a different kind of body." Gloria nudged Meg and looked pointedly toward the kitchen.

Meg snickered. "I see the lady prefers a full-bodied darker roast. Perhaps the title of Mrs. Muffin Man is in the near future?"

Kathryn lifted her mug to her lips to mask the scorching in her cheeks. Marriage looked good on her friends. Meg and her computer expert hubby Eli had married first. Then Gloria and Pastor Owen wed just last month in a beautiful May ceremony, beating their friends Kim and Officer Jackson to the altar by a week. Emma and Ben's wedding was this fall. One by one, all her friends had made their relationships permanent. It was like a real-life version of the old song, The Farmer in the Dell. Each man picked a wife.

Except hers.

That made her the cheese that stood alone.

Kathryn averted her gaze. She'd never felt pressure to tie the knot, but now that they were the only ones left unhitched . . . the coffee turned bitter in her mouth. It left an uncomfortably similar feeling to never being the chosen wife in the grade school version of the game. Every pot didn't find its lid. Even Scripture said there were all sorts of dishes and bowls in the kitchen. Some were made of precious metals, others of wood and clay. Some were saved for special occasions, others for ordinary use.

Ethan clattered in the kitchen, and his movements drew her attention like a meme from a video gone viral. When he noticed her watching him, his expression lit up, and Kathryn felt anything but ordinary. Her insides tap danced when he looked at her like that. Ethan dusted his hands on the front of his apron and hurried to their table. She tingled as he dropped a kiss on her forehead. "All done filming?"

"I think so." Kathryn smiled up at him, and her skin cracked. Cringing, she patted her dried-out, makeup-covered jawline. She always had to layer it on thick for filming. Tugging off her magnetic false eyelashes, she rooted around in her bag for a pre-moistened facial wipe. "I need to get this makeup off."

Ethan squeezed her shoulder. "You're gorgeous au natural."

Meg elbowed Gloria. "That's service with a smile."

"More than a smile," Gloria snorted.

Kathryn glared at her friends and swiped the cleansing tissue across her forehead. Even though she'd known Ethan since they were kids at summer camp, her middle still got all mushy when he touched her. It made her feel like the tastiest item on his menu. Maybe her man had a wife in mind after all?

"You might prefer me makeup free, but social media is a cruel and unforgiving employer."

"No kidding," Meg sniffed. "Did you hear about that writer complaining about how hard it is to maintain a healthy lifestyle while traveling?"

"Is that the guy from *Eating on the Road*?" Ethan leaned a hip against the table, in no hurry to get back to the kitchen. He folded his arms across his chest. His long-sleeved T-shirt did nothing to conceal the lean contours of his frame. She might have lovingly dubbed him her muffin man, but he was nothing like the tubby nursery rhyme character. Ethan was long limbed, broad shouldered, and all smiles, and knew—of course—who it was that Meg referenced. He followed a ton of foodies on social media.

Meg nodded. "He partnered with the nutritionist from *Killing Carbs*. They created easy recipes that only required the supplies found in a standard hotel room to cook."

Uh oh. Kathryn could just imagine how wrong that could go—an influencer's worse nightmare. Her gut flipped. She'd seen something in her news feed about steaming a chicken breast using a coffee maker.

Gloria giggled. "*#EatingRoadKill* is trending. People are posting images of the failed recipes."

Hijacked hashtags were the worst. There was no way for a content creator to control it once it went viral. Her friends didn't understand.

Both ridiculously huge missteps and small, poorly crafted posts could send brands trending for all the wrong reasons. There were no backsies on the internet. All publicity isn't good publicity, especially when your life's work is rebranded as *Eating Road Kill* by feverish followers. One negative connection like that could sink Kathryn, and everything she'd worked for would be gone.

"Kathryn?"

Ethan touched her arm, and she jerked. By her friends' stares, she realized she'd missed something.

"Are you okay?"

"Better than okay." Kathryn beamed the ray of artificial sunshine everyone expected from her. Anything less and she might as well axe her show herself. "But I'm afraid I missed what you said. My mind . . ." She flapped her hand.

Meg's hand dropped and rested protectively across her middle.

Kathryn's heart fluttered. "Are you?" Her gaze lowered to Meg's belly, then darted to Gloria, who was nodding, before landing back on Meg. "Are you pregnant?"

"Yes!" Meg squealed.

Kathryn shot to her feet and threw her arms around her friend. "That's wonderful!"

Outwardly, Kathryn did all the right things. She smiled, laughed, and wiped the corners of her damp eyes. But inside, another narrative played. If Meg was pregnant, it wouldn't be long before the others caught baby fever and their social circle moved from coffee shops to playgrounds. Her body quivered, but with none of the earlier delightful notes. This time, the sourness sank deep. Like the last kid waiting to be picked, dread clawed up her spine. The cheese stood alone, indeed.

The bells over the door jingled again, and Gloria's eyes bugged. Her gasp was sharper than the social media comments on Eating Road Kill.

Kathryn turned, and Tiffany Duthie gave an awkward wave.

Cringing, Kathryn's inner quaking morphed into waves. Tiff was part of a scandal that framed Gloria years ago. It involved a bogus drug study that was nearly approved for human trials on the residents of Life House, a local women's shelter their friend, Kim, ran. Meg lived at Life House for her first year in Sycamore Hill, and she took Tiff's reckless endangerment of the residents personally.

Tiff wasn't supposed to be here. Not yet. Not today.

A hesitant smile replaced Tiff's usual confident grin: a smile directed at Kathryn, not Gloria.

No, no, no, no, no.

Plausible reasons for her and Tiff knowing each other failed to gel. All Kathryn could think of was the truth, and the truth was not an option.

Meg stepped closer to Gloria and wrapped a protective arm around her quivering shoulders. "What do you want?"

Tiff's eyes widened and Kathryn gave her head a small shake.

Slumping ever-so-slightly, Tiff flicked her attention to Gloria. "Hi."

That was all she said. One word. And Kathryn's chest squeezed like she was hooked up to Ethan's juicer. She couldn't think. Couldn't breathe. She wasn't ready.

Tiff just showed up. That wasn't the plan. What good was a plan if a person didn't stick to it? Kathryn needed time. Tiff was supposed to give her a heads up. She was supposed to tell her when and where it would go down, not just *appear*.

Sure, Kathryn hadn't answered Tiff's message. But she didn't know how, and that didn't mean Tiff could just arrive.

Okay. *Messages*. Plural. There wasn't just one. And Kathryn did reply. She just hadn't answered the part about Tiff coming to Sycamore Hill, because that could ruin everything.

"I'm here to explain." Tiff jammed her hands into

her front pockets. What she needed to explain didn't need clarifying. Everyone in Sycamore Hill knew Tiff Duthie's scheming had cost Gloria her university degree. Add that to the fact Meg was personally invested in the ministry of Life House, and Tiff was lucky this welcome wagon didn't run her down.

A muscle pulsed in Gloria's jaw.

Tiff's gaze darted to Kathryn and bounced back to Gloria, but not before Kathryn saw the disappointment in it. Tiff would never disclose how they knew each other. It would violate the code, which meant Kathryn's secret was safe.

For now.

Kathryn dampened her lips. How was she going to play this?

"I saw you sneak into Kim's wedding." Meg bought Kathryn more time to think. "I can't believe after everything you tried to do to Life House—to her—you crashed her wedding."

Tiff blinked rapidly and turned her face away. She swallowed. She needed support, that was clear. But that wasn't Kathryn's responsibility. There were tons of other people she could call on after she left The Muffin Man. It didn't have to be Kathryn. Pulling Kathryn into it had to be a conflict of interest.

"I didn't realize it was a wedding until it was too late." Tiff's lips folded in until they disappeared.

Tiff's eyes found Kathryn again. At least she thought

they did. It felt like they did, but she wasn't about to lift her gaze and confirm it.

Hi-ho, the derry-o, Kathryn didn't want Tiff to choose her. So, she stared at Ethan's carefully constructed window display. She blinked until the pressure behind her eyes lessened. Helping Tiff wasn't optional. Kathryn knew that she'd help. But not until she figured out how to do it without destroying her life.

Kathryn squared her shoulders. "I should film the next segment."

Gloria perked, looking just as eager as Kathryn felt to get away. "Yes." Gloria slung her purse strap over her shoulder. "Let's go. I have nothing to say to that woman."

That woman. Gloria spat it as if even saying Tiff's name would sully her. Gloria's eagerness to escape and Tiff's devastated posture heaped guilt upon guilt. Gloria thought Kathryn was helping her leave with dignity, but Kathryn was using her. Kathryn was the one who needed to escape.

Kathryn threw a small smile to Ethan, who nodded encouragingly. He thought she was protecting Gloria, too. Shame heated her cheeks. She held her breath until the bells over the door jingled as it swung closed behind them. Guilt crushed her chest.

When a fellow addict reached out, you didn't walk away.

Chapter Two

"Do you want to talk about it?" Ethan flipped a bakery chair and rested its seat on the table so Kathryn could sweep the broom underneath. He'd locked the bakery doors a half hour ago, and when Kathryn showed up to help him close, he'd sent Meg home early. Meg was pursuing her Landscape Architect Degree and had a paper due tomorrow. She could use the extra time to work on her assignment.

Kathryn's expression pinched. She slogged through the evening routine with none of her usual joviality.

Ethan had debated all day on whether he should bring up Tiff's arrival. He'd noticed Kathryn's reaction to the woman. He'd almost convinced himself he'd imagined it, until Kathryn showed up with red-rimmed eyes. Tiff's reappearance had upset her.

"Talk about what?" Kathryn cocked her head with an expression of innocence. She'd pulled her hair into a ponytail and scrubbed of the heavy film makeup. He liked her better like this, clean and fresh like the girl he remembered from their summer camp days.

He kept flipping chairs, tracking her from the corner of his eye. She reminded him of the baby deer they'd befriended at camp. The poor thing was tangled in some fencing and didn't know it needed help. When they came at it directly, it fought them. It took them over thirty minutes to convince the deer that they were friendly. Finally, it stilled and let them free its legs, but the entire time its eyes stretched wide and afraid.

Just like Kathryn. A direct approach would make her bolt.

"We should talk about Tiffany." With no more chairs to flip, he puttered around, keeping her in his peripheral vision.

Kathryn puckered her lips and resumed sweeping with enough force that he was pretty sure he'd have to add a new broom to the weekly shopping list.

"Do you know her?" Ethan straightened the sugar canisters and the disposable stir sticks. Everything was in its place, just as it should be.

"We all know Tiff."

He frowned at her non-answer.

"I got her on film, crashing Kim's wedding. Remember? I spoke to her that day."

Kathryn had a strong reaction to Tiff then, as well. He'd seen the uncut wedding footage. When Tiff entered late, Kathryn's usual steady hand trembled.

He was about to challenge her when the bakery door rattled. The dead bolt held secure, but the string of bells resting against the top third of the glass bounced noisily. Ethan separated the slats in the blinds, and his mom grinned back at him.

Ethan unlocked the door and swung it open. "What are you doing here?" He pulled his mother into a hug. Looking over her shoulder, he grinned at his dad, who followed her into the bakery. His parents lived in Grander, and despite it only being a little more than thirty minutes away, they didn't visit often, and never unannounced. Ethan chalked it up to his dad's discomfort with Ethan's chosen profession. Dad liked his men to be men, and having a baker for a son was a tender spot. But Dad was trying.

"We were in the area," Mom said. "You've been gushing about the new coffee roaster, and we saw the lights were still on." She shrugged. "We took a chance."

"Hi, Mr. and Mrs. Roberts." Kathryn returned the broom to the cleaning closet and flipped down the bar stools that lined the counter separating the new coffee roaster from the dining area. Her stiff movements had relaxed now that their conversation about Tiff had been interrupted.

Mom hugged Kathryn, pulled back, slid her hands down Kathryn's arms, and squeezed Kathryn's fingers before letting go, not-so-subtly feeling Kathryn's empty ring finger.

Ethan glared at her, and she blew him an air kiss.

He kneaded the tight muscles in his shoulder. If Mom was any more obvious, Kathryn might notice her family heirloom ring was missing from her finger. Then he could kiss good-bye any chance of surprising her with a romantic, web-show worthy proposal.

Not that he had a romantic, web-show worthy proposal idea to implement. Kathryn was the creative one, and he could hardly ask her for ideas.

"That's an impressive piece of machinery." Dad's low whistle of appreciation shot confidence through Ethan.

Kathryn flicked on the recessed lights Ethan had installed above the roasting area. "The roaster was delivered last week. Ethan's been trying out recipes and blends ever since."

Ethan puffed like pastry under her praise. She really was the cream in his coffee. They were better together.

"Who'd have thought Betty Crocker would need experience as a machinist." Dad laughed at his own joke.

Mom smoothed a hand down the front of her shirt, but Ethan noticed how it trembled. Despite saying for months that Dad really was proud of Ethan but didn't know how to connect with him, her involuntary reactions undermined her claims. Where was this effort that Mom spoke of? It certainly wasn't in calling him Betty Crocker.

Ethan deflated. Things were better with his dad than they used to be, but those little digs still hurt. His construction-working father never accepted that it took more than muscles and a refusal to cry to make a man.

Mom folded her hands in her lap and squared her shoulders. "We also stopped in to share some exciting news." She looked pointedly at Dad.

"Your mother and I invested in property in Northern Ontario."

"You're retiring?" A strange mixture of sadness and relief threw Ethan off balance.

"That's the dream."

Kathryn clasped her hands to her chest. "I've always wanted to see the Northern Lights."

Kathryn's enthusiasm bought Ethan a few extra minutes. She really was the soft creamy filling holding together two brittle wafers.

"We aren't moving there," Mom said. "At least, not yet. It'll be a vacation rental for now. There's a bit more paperwork to sign, but we wanted to tell you in person. And we wanted to see this." She gestured to the roaster. "It's quite the contraption. I love how it is right here, in the dining area." Mom's light, bubbly voice overcompensated for Dad's lack of enthusiasm. All the effort to connect came from Mom. Just like always.

"Ethan had to move the counter out a few extra feet to make room." Kathryn looped her arm through his. "Now he can host coffee tours, and it makes his business stand out from the chain stores popping up all over the place."

"You moved the counter out?" Dad checked out his work, seeming equally doubtful and impressed. Clearly it mattered little that Ethan had worked with his dad's construction company throughout most of high school.

"How does the roaster work?" Mom angled herself away from Dad.

"This is the drum." Ethan gestured to the machine's core, ignoring his dad's question. "The beans go in here, kind of like a front load washing machine. As the drum spins, the beans roast."

"It must smell heavenly in here."

Kathryn grinned. "Even the people who don't enjoy the taste of coffee have been drawn into the bakery. It's quite the magnet."

"The chaff comes out here." Ethan slid out the trap over a galvanized bucket.

"What are the probes?" Mom pointed to two metal rods.

"They track the roasting time. They're connected to my laptop, which runs an artisan software to track the first and second crack. Then, the beans cool in this spinner." Ethan pointed to the round basin that had an arm that spun to move the beans. It looked like a large mixing bowl.

"Cracks?" That was all his dad said. One word, lifted at the end to make it a question. Ethan should be thankful he was even listening.

"The first crack is when the moisture releases from the bean. If I stopped then, it would make a light roast. The second crack is when the cell structure breaks down. It creates a dark roast."

"I'm so proud of you." His mom fussed like always, but it wasn't enough.

For once, Ethan would like to make his dad proud. But things between them never shifted back to normal after Ethan announced his plans to attend culinary school and then apprentice under a local baker. His dad had assumed the kitchen was a phase, and Ethan would eventually work with him. When it finally sunk in that he'd never hand his business down to his son, Dad didn't speak to him for a month. But that was all in the past, according to Mom, the queen of excuses.

Dad was embarrassed. Ethan was determined. His mom was torn.

"Did you catch the game last night?" Dad addressed Kathryn. He'd stopped asking Ethan those kinds of questions years ago.

"Wouldn't miss it! That hit in the last inning—"

"I know. Incredible. He's only eighteen. Did you know that?"

And that was that. Ethan checked his watch. Dad was done with the bakery in less than five minutes. Four minutes longer than usual.

As Kathryn and Dad bantered, Ethan swallowed disappointment so bitter there wasn't a treat in the shop that could sweeten his gut. He loved that Kathryn could talk sports with his dad. The man needed someone to quip with over stats, hits, and scores. God must have been off his game when he gave a man that was all sports metaphors and muscle a son that was spices and frosting.

"You'll turn my boy into a man yet." Dad slugged Kathryn on the upper arm and bellowed at something she'd said.

Ethan looked away.

He was glad Kathryn and Dad got along. Really, he was.

His mom poked Dad hard.

He straightened and swung his gaze back to Ethan. "Looks like a big investment."

"Yeah." Ethan scratched the back of his neck. "I'm banking everything on it. Chain stores are crushing small businesses like me. I needed something to set me apart, and no one is roasting locally."

"The closest thing is the guy roasting beans in his garage and selling the fresh product to restaurants," Kathryn said. "But he's closer to Grander than Sycamore Hill."

"I went to his place to see about ordering local coffee," Ethan added, "and smelling the roasting beans firsthand convinced me. I didn't want to just sell local product; I wanted my customers to see and smell the process."

Mom's forehead wrinkled. "What does he think of your venture?"

Ethan shrugged. "I didn't meet him. He was out on a delivery. His girlfriend showed me around."

"Ethan's not infringing on his business," Kathryn clarified. "Ethan's not supplying restaurants. He's only roasting for his customers." She beamed at him. "He's going to offer coffee tastings, and we even discussed setting up a coffee delivery system where customers can order freshly roasted beans to be delivered weekly."

Ethan snagged a few baked goods from the front display and set them on the counter while Kathryn bragged on his marketing ideas.

His dad lifted his chin. "Out of all the things you could invest in, why coffee? Why not something more secure, like property?"

"You mean property in Northern Ontario?"

"Real estate is always a safe bet. It'll generate a nice passive income for your mother and me. Even Kathryn wants to see the Northern Lights. People will rent from us. You'll see."

"I think coffee is a secure, solid investment, and it makes sense for me. Nearly everybody drinks coffee, and nearly every food-based business sells it. Roasting it is the next logical step."

"It's brilliant." It was subtle, but Kathryn moved closer and stood with him. She tipped her face up and flashed that megawatt smile he loved. "He'll make a killing."

Dad grunted. "The boy could never kill anything. Remember when we went hunting that time?"

Ethan snorted. Mom could say all she wanted that Dad was proud, but pudding's missing ingredient was proof.

"Grant." His mom's tone carried a warning, and when her gaze shifted to Ethan's, it softened with an apology. "How are you going to beat the prices of the chain store?"

Ethan let his dad's barb go. It wasn't Mom's fault that he and Dad repelled each other like vanilla extract and mosquitoes. "I can't, so I'm not going to try. Real coffee lovers think of chain-store coffee like a fine chef thinks of fast food. I'm catering to a higher breed of coffee drinker."

"The coffee snobs?"

Kathryn lifted her chin. "We prefer to think of them as discerning customers that know a good product when they taste it."

His parents looked unconvinced. To them, Ethan would always be the little league dreamer picking dandelions in right field, oblivious to the game unfolding on the diamond. Pressure built behind his eyes until he could feel his heartbeat in his skull. When he looked at Kathryn, it intensified.

She put the pastries Ethan had retrieved on plates and handed each of his parents one, taking the pressure and focus off him. Then she changed the conversation. "Did you hear that my web show is up for a Fan Favourite Choice Award?"

Ethan's breath stalled. How didn't he know this? "You are?"

"I've never heard of that." Mom took a delicate bite of the pastry.

Kathryn's eyes danced. "My book agent confirmed it

today, and I agreed to let my name stand." She looked at him. "I was planning on telling you tonight."

Ethan hugged her. "That's amazing!" He whispered the words into her hair. "Maybe this will lead to another cookbook deal."

Kathryn's eyes sparkled. "That's the hope."

"What exactly is this award?" Mom asked.

"It's a contest that takes place on social media. Fans vote for their favorite social media channel over the next few weeks. *Sycamore Hill at Sunrise* has a pretty good following, so I'm hopeful." Kathryn lifted a shoulder as if it were no big deal, except Ethan knew that it was.

He pressed another kiss to her temple. "Win or lose, you're always a winner to me."

"Good luck," Dad said.

"Sounds exciting," Mom added.

Except it wasn't. Kathryn hated popularity contests, and now she'd announced it to his parents, they'd be hounding her for updates. Their gazes tangled. She offered him a soft smile and the pressure that had been behind his eyes dropped to his chest and sucked the air out of him like a fallen soufflé. She'd thrown herself on the sword to save him, and he loved her for it.

Chapter Three

Kathryn stood between the diner's double doors in Grander and shook the rain out of her umbrella before folding it closed.

"Kathryn?"

Ethan's parents were leaving the diner as she entered. His mom gave her a quick hug.

"Grant, Shannon, what a surprise!" Kathryn looked past them to glance at the man standing behind them wearing an expensive looking business suit. He looked pointedly at his watch and bounced a briefcase off his shin.

Yeah, yeah, time is money. Kathryn ignored him.

Shannon squeezed her hands. "We just signed the papers for that investment property we told you about. What are you doing here?"

"I got a tip that Grander's mayor is making some sort of announcement that will impact Sycamore Hill. It's supposed to happen in front of the diner later this morning. I'm recording it for my show, you know"—she winked—"to drum up some votes."

The all-work-and-no-play suit gestured as if to usher them out the door.

"Wait." Kathryn dug into her purse for her phone. "Let me grab a snapshot of us. I have to post more content now that I'm in that contest." Kathryn flipped the camera into selfie mode and Ethan's parents huddled around her. She snapped the photo and quickly checked it. "It's perfect." She pointed to their business advisor in the background. "I'll blur you out," she promised.

"Thanks." As he dipped his head and looked at his watch again, a muscle in his jaw twitched. The suit was impatient.

They said goodbye, and Kathryn claimed a booth by the window as a waitress approached. The suit walked Mr. and Mrs. Roberts to their vehicle, despite the continuing drizzle of rain.

"I'll have a coffee, please." Kathryn dropped her gaze to the waitress's nameplate. "Thanks, Gabby."

Tiff Duthie slid onto the bench seat across from her. "And can I get a black coffee, please?"

"Sure thing." Gabby hurried off.

Tiff eyed the diner with a frown. "Any special reason we're meeting in Grander? I'm staying at the Sycamore Inn, and The Muffin Man is way nicer than this."

Gabby reappeared at the table with two thick ceramic mugs and a bowl of creamers.

Kathryn waited for the waitress to leave. Any special reason? Yeah. How about not wanting to be seen with the woman who'd hurt her friends. Wrapping her hands around the warm ceramic, Kathryn tugged the mug closer to her and let the wafting steam heat her face. Once Gabby left, she met Tiff's eyes. "Why'd you just show up at the bakery like that? The plan was to wait until I was ready."

"You'd been avoiding me. You were never going to be ready."

Kathryn sighed heavily and with exaggeration. "That's not what we agreed upon."

Tiff made a noise in her throat. "My sobriety is not about you. It's about me working the steps. This is my next step. And whether you're ready or not, I have to take it." Tiff's confident air lost its edge. She relaxed her posture and traced the rim of her mug with her fingertip. "But I was kind of hoping you'd act as my sponsor while I was in Sycamore Hill."

"Sponsor?" Kathryn sat back. Well, she didn't just sit back. She pressed against the vinyl-covered bench seat back as deeply as she could. She could not be Tiff's sponsor. Not in a million years. She bounced a curled knuckle against her thigh, her cheeks no longer comfortably warm but scorching.

"I have some apologies to make," Tiff continued, "and I don't expect them to be well received. But even if they aren't, trying will go a long way in keeping my relationship with God right."

That's when it hit Kathryn, hard enough she would have staggered had she been standing. *Tiff didn't know.* Her mouth dried up. Kathryn swallowed a gulp of coffee, yet the hot liquid failed to wet her whistle. "Nobody in Sycamore Hill knows about my past."

Tiff's mouth slackened.

Yup. Shocked.

Tiff rubbed absently at her arms. "You grew up in Sycamore Hill. How is that possible?"

Kathryn dumped a creamer into the coffee and studied its pleasant, swirling pattern. "You've heard my story. My drinking didn't get out of hand until I went away for university. My parents never told anyone."

Because they were ashamed.

Thankfully, her parents didn't live in Sycamore Hill anymore, having retired to their cottage years ago. Distance would spare them certain humiliation if Tiff's appearance outed the secret they'd worked so hard to keep hidden.

Kathryn was so familiar with feelings of shame, she could put it on like a favorite sweater. She kept her attention fixed on the pearly white cream trailing through the dark liquid.

Tiff studied her for a long, quiet moment. "I take the anonymous part seriously. I would never tell anyone about your addiction."

The weight on her chest lifted. Her secret was safe.

"But secrets can be triggers for relapse."

Who did Tiff think she was, lecturing her on sobriety? Kathryn had been clean years longer than Tiff. Besides, Tiff wasn't her sponsor. Kathryn didn't even have one anymore, and she was doing just fine. Before her last sponsor moved away, she'd told Kathryn it was the nudge Kathryn needed to shift from the meetings in Grander to the one in the Sycamore Hill Community Church basement. But Kathryn couldn't do it. She couldn't seem to make the leap from out-of-town-nobody to local-celeb-in-rehab. She knew she needed to. She even planned to. Someday. But who said someday had to be now?

"I was reading Luke 8:7 this morning."

Kathryn read no judgment in Tiff's expression. Only concern.

"Secrets will be brought into the open. Everything concealed will be brought to light and made known to all."

Kathryn's insides turned over, her stunned silence assuring Tiff the point had landed. Kathryn didn't want everyone to know. And if Tiff wasn't trying to draw Kathryn into her recovery, they'd never have to know. At least, not yet.

Tiff lifted her coffee mug and grimaced a bit of a know-it-all smile over the rim. "When you expose a secret, it loses its power. I should know."

Yes, she should. Kathryn had heard her story several times in support meetings. Tiff's secret addiction during her final university years is what started her descent. Before long, she was piling sin upon sin to feed her cravings. Accepting the pharmaceutical company's bribe to skew drug study results was the tipping point. Mostly because it implicated Gloria, her project partner. Guilt eventually led Tiff to rehab where she fought to get clean while Gloria fought to clear her name.

"I'm only staying in town long enough to make my apologies," Tiff said. "But knowing I could call on you when it gets rough would mean a lot."

When, not if.

Tiff accepted that it was going to be difficult, but she was doing the right thing anyway. Kathryn admired that about her. She could see why she and Gloria had once been good friends. When the girl was in, she was all in.

"Of course, you can call me." She said the right words but prayed she wouldn't have to live them out. Just the idea of it made her brain hurt.

Tiff grinned. "Thanks."

Kathryn knew the struggle Tiff faced. She'd followed the same path when she tracked down her university mates, the ones who exposed her drinking and arranged an intervention. Kathryn had said and done some awful things to them, and they had deserved to know that she'd turned her life around and that God eventually used their brave decision to change her.

But none of that happened within Sycamore Hill's town limits. No part of her old life followed her when she moved home, and she wasn't interested in revealing it now. Not when the entire community and internet world would be watching her and voting on whether they liked her. Social media was a fickle friend. People had been cancelled for less. But none of that was Tiff's fault. "I'll be here for you," Kathryn resolved, then looked at her watch. "Oh, it's almost time for the mayor's announcement. I need to get out there."

"You're recording yourself?"

"I connect my tablet to my phone's data to livestream and manage it with a remote."

"Let me help. It's the least I can do."

After throwing some cash on the table to cover the bill and tip, they set up out front. The rain had stopped, and the occasional ray of sunlight broke through the clouds. It was strange no one else gathered for the announcement. Kathryn opened the private message sent to her through her social media account. She double-checked the location and time. Maybe she'd get an exclusive? She tried to figure out the identity of the fan that sent the tip so she could thank them, but the account was under a pseudonym. She'd try again later.

Positioning herself so the light hit her from the front, Kathryn rotated her torso to a pleasing angle and beamed her high-wattage smile.

Tiff pointed at her from behind the lens to indicate they were rolling.

"Hello, Sycamore Hill. I'm live in Grander, waiting for the mayor, who is rumored to be making an announcement soon. This announcement is alleged to have a strong Sycamore Hill connection, and it looks like I've got the exclusive."

An engine roared behind her. Kathryn's scalp prickled, but years of training prevented her from turning until Tiff's steady hold on the tablet dipped just enough to reveal her huge, expanding, saucer-sized eyes. Kathryn shifted as a wall of cold wet hit her from behind. She shrieked.

Tiff pointed the tablet at the vehicle racing away, and then slowly turned back to a dripping Kathryn, who was now peeling her blouse from her skin with two fingers. Muddy streaks ran down her body. Her hair was plastered to the nape of her neck. Swiping a hand across her face, she pulled it away and looked at it. Black mascara. All captured live for her viewing audience. Her mouth sagged open, and for the first time in her entire career, she had no words. Nada. Zip.

Tiff turned the lens to face her. "That's all for now. This is Tiff Duthie, signing off for Kathryn Withers." She ended the video.

Kathryn rushed into the diner just as Gabby was coming out with a checkered tea towel. "I saw what that car did. Awful! It was like he aimed right for you." She handed the towel to Kathryn.

"Thanks." Kathryn twisted her hair to squeeze out the water. She mentally reviewed the items in the trunk of her car. She always had a change of clothes, but she wasn't sure she had time to reapply her make up. A slick, wet bun would have to do for her hair. "Do you know how long we have until the mayor makes his announcement?"

Gabby blinked several times. "What announcement? The mayor isn't scheduled to be here."

The ache in the back of her throat soured. She'd been set up. This was bad. So, so bad. The muffled ring spilling out of her purse intensified when she pulled it out. The cell displayed her agent's name. Kathryn's regular cooking segment produced such popular recipes that she'd landed an agent who sold her cookbook to a medium-sized publisher.

"Kathryn." Heather didn't wait. She started talking as soon as Kathryn answered. "I'm glad I caught you. I heard from the publisher. They agree that the contest is great press, not only for the cookbook, but also for the coffee book you pitched."

Kathryn put the phone on speaker and set it on the nearest table. She continued to wring out her hair. "That's great." A notification popped up on her screen. Someone had posted a video of her and tagged her.

Heather's prattle faded. Kathryn's fingers twitched as she tapped the notification and muted the video's sound. An anonymous account had already reposted the livestream just taken outside. It captured the vehicle deliberately veering to hit a puddle and drench her. The poster set the speed to slow motion, accentuating every micro-expression of Kathryn's.

She spun. Tiff.

No, she still spoke with Gabby.

Kathryn squinted and looked across the street.

Nothing lurked in the bushes. No one lingered.

The caption under the video read: *Small-town girl stages a fake event in the city.*

Fake?

"Kathryn? Are you there?"

Right, her agent. The book. "Yes, I am. Sorry, it's just a surprise. I figured the publisher wasn't interested in the coffee book."

"They weren't, at first. But when they heard about your nomination, they came up with a publicity plan that benefits everyone."

That pitch in Kathryn's heart twisted and stabbed. She replayed the video, muted, of course. Speaking of publicity . . .

"Imagine this: a camera follows you to capture the opening days of Ethan's roasting business. Viewers will see it all, the good, the bad, and the crazy. It'll give you more screen time, publicity for Ethan's business, and generate votes. Your gentle, self-deprecating humour has always been a hit."

Ethan needed the press. And it would solidify her next book, netting Heather a nice commission. It was a win for everyone.

Everyone but her. That fist always squeezing her lungs might as well rip them out of her chest. She'd never be able to breathe again if a camera followed her around 24/7.

Heather kept talking. "The other finalists have already started drumming up support on social media."

Had they also started their smear campaigns against competitors? Was that why she was here, dripping wet?

"Do you have someone that can film for you?"

"Yes," Kathryn answered automatically. Gloria would do it if she asked.

Heather babbled on about what a great opportunity this was and how all press was good press.

Kathryn snorted. Clearly, Heather hadn't seen the latest.

"Livestream is the best."

Kathryn jerked. "Live?"

"Yes, the unedited stuff is exploding online."

Impossible. Never in a million years. Not gonna happen.

Kathryn was really careful. She only let people see the parts of herself she wanted to share. If they saw the mess that existed outside the camera's frame, if they learned about her past, she'd not only kiss winning the contest good-bye, but also her show, and maybe even Ethan. She didn't doubt his love for her, but tons of girls had the hots for Ethan. Her followers were always dishing about him. And once he realized what a train wreck she was, he'd cut her loose. He had to. It was what any sane guy would do.

It wouldn't matter that her viewers called their reunion fate or referred to Ethan as the Ken to her Barbie or the peanut butter to her jelly. It wouldn't matter that she'd featured him on her show to make up for acciden-tally ruining a huge advertising campaign two Christmases ago. It wouldn't matter they'd been back together ever since.

"Did you hear me, Kathryn?"

"Yes, it's great. Thank you." Kathryn hung up. She'd send an apology email to Heather later. In all her Sunrise episodes and even in her short midday reels, people only saw the tiniest part of her. The perfect part. Because if her viewers saw the real her, they'd chew her up and spit her out faster than the flopped #EatingRoadKill disaster.

But what would be crueller, what she couldn't stomach, was the possibility that if she stopped being social media's sweetheart, Ethan might finally see the ugliest parts of her. And worse, reject her because of them.

Chapter Four

"Thanks for being my guinea pigs." Ethan rubbed his palms together as he stood behind the high counter in the bakery. Kathryn, Meg, her husband, Eli, and his business partner, Addison, sat on the barstools opposite the roaster. "I want to practice the tour before I start booking appointments."

"What exactly is a roasting tour?" Eli spun on his stool, ignoring the way Meg frowned at his childish action. Eli and Addison rented office space above the Muffin Man, where they engineered speciality computer software for various companies. They'd sold their most successful program to the town. It was a program they'd developed for Meg to use for a school project, but then they expanded the idea to streamline city permit applications of all kinds. The guys were more than happy to take a break and consume free coffee, and Eli loved any excuse to come down to the bakery and flirt with his wife.

The door rattled.

Ethan hurried to it and undid the deadbolt. "Sorry, we're not open yet."

"Your online hours say you are," the man huffed.

"Yes, we usually are, but I posted a notice that today we are filming a promotional clip and we'll open late." Ethan fished around in his front pocket and handed the man his card. "Come back later with this, and I'll give you a coffee on the house."

The man accepted the card with a grunt. He didn't appear placated. A bronze coffee mug pin on his lapel glinted in the light.

"I'll make it a punch card and give you five free coffees on me."

"Thanks for nothing." His grip on the door released.

Ethan double-checked that the sign he taped to the outside of the door was still there before rejoining his friends.

"When did you start offering a punch card?" Kathryn appeared genuinely surprised.

Ethan winked. "Just now."

"Ah," Addison cleared his throat, interrupting their exchange. "I came for the coffee, but I'm not too sure about the camera." He tipped his head toward the camera in Gloria's hands and frowned.

"The camera's your friend, Addison." Gloria lowered

the lens and matched Addison frown for frown, but the corners of her lips twitched with playfulness. "Maybe Sarah will see it and decide she needs to be part of the Sycamore Hill social scene."

Ethan grinned as Addison's cheeks reddened. Addison met Sarah when he went to a tech conference in the city. Addison had visited her once in Glory River, but the official word was they were friends. Neither was ready to relocate for the other. Still, Ethan got the feeling the local girls paled in comparison for this guy.

"Since I can't get out of filming live," Kathryn explained to the group. "I appreciate your willingness to participate and take the pressure of me. Ignore Gloria as she films. I'll use the footage to drum up interest for Ethan's new venture."

"And generate votes for you for the contest." Gloria looked pointedly at Kathryn.

Kathryn waved off Gloria's comment. "Ethan will teach us about coffee, its history, and how to roast it. It's like a product tour. You'll know everything there is to know about coffee by the time we are done."

Kathryn gave them a few last-minute tips about acting natural, and when Gloria pointed the device their way, Kathryn transformed. She came alive like a second personality emerged. Her alter ego was confident, vibrant, and relaxed in a way core-Kathryn rarely presented. She even spoke differently, prolonging her vowel sounds. But as fun as camera-Kathryn was, Ethan loved the real Kathryn best.

"Hey friends." Kathryn batted her false eyelashes. "I have big news. Most of you know about my cookbook, *Move over, Betty, There's a New Crockpot in Town*, and I'm excited to tell you about my upcoming coffee roasting book! Part of my research involves trying out new flavors, understanding the roasting process, and immersing myself into coffee culture—which is a real thing. I mean, it's bigger than Barkitecture."

"Barkitecture?"

Gloria briefly panned to Addison to capture his confused expression.

"I did an entire Sunrise segment on the growing popularity of designing gorgeous indoor spaces for pets. Surely, you saw it?" Kathryn's slow drawl and cute gestures communicated that she didn't expect Addison to have seen the show. Her ability to downplay herself and her expectations on her audience was part of her charm.

Ethan snuck a glance at his phone, which he placed on the counter screen-side up, so he could track Kathryn's viewers. Every second, more people tuned in, and their comments floated up the side of his screen.

I love barkitecture!

Congrats on the book deal.

What's the title of the new book?

Fabulous episode. I transformed a closet for my dog.

Where did you buy your shirt?

"Let me introduce Ethan Roberts. Ethan, tell them a bit about yourself."

I've been to his bakery.

Last time I was there, some guy bumfuzzled the staff. Messed up my order.

Ethan flipped his phone so the comments wouldn't distract him while he addressed the camera. "I own an artisan bakery and coffee roasting business in Sycamore Hill called The Muffin Man."

Kathryn poked her head into the shot. "And ya'll know him as my better half." She winked before taking her seat at the counter. Kathryn typed a comment into her phone and left it, screen up, on the counter. It took all of Ethan's self-control not to let his attention drop to it.

Ethan placed four tiny mugs on the counter, one in front of each of them, while addressing the online audience. "I hope you'll come and enjoy the robust and full-bodied flavours coming your way from The Muffin Man."

"This is the only time I'm ever embracing a full body." Kathryn ran a hand down her slender side and clucked her tongue. "The camera adds too many pounds."

"Thankfully, I don't live on camera." Meg bantered perfectly. "Can I put cream in mine?"

Meg hadn't seen the online comment about the messed-up orders. That was the day Meg's volatile ex showed up to harass her. A few orders were delayed, a couple more mixed up. Ethan did what he could to make the customers happy, but Meg's safety had been the real priority.

Ethan set a little creamer on the counter in front of Meg. "Did you know that black coffee came from the Arab world? When Europeans wanted to be separate from the Arabs, they added milk to lighten the darkness." Ethan dribbled a trail of coffee beans across the counter as he spoke.

"Ahh, Ethan? Are these beans past their best before date?" Kathryn rolled a green bean between her index finger and thumb.

Gloria adjusted the camera angle.

He chuckled. "Coffee beans are supposed to be green. They are seeds that grow inside a cherry, which is a fruit."

"For real?" Ethan loved the way Eli leaned in with genuine interest.

"Each cherry has two seeds inside, and depending on where they grow, they can produce coffee beans with natural flavours of cinnamon, mango, or pecan."

Kathryn's screen lit up, and Ethan snuck a glance.

No way!

I didn't know that.

Kathryn had responded to the negative comment.

Bonus points for the word bumfuzzled. Impressive. *Shoot me a DM and I'll arrange a tour, on me.*

And that was it. The heart emojis were all over her response. But she wasn't done charming her audience.

"The audience has some comments." Kathryn read from the screen. "*Brewlover* writes, Coffee's a fruit? That's the best news I've ever heard. *AllNatural* wonders if coffee can count toward our recommended daily servings of fruit? And *AllAboutTheKids* wants to know what makes for a fruitier flavor."

Kathryn's allure and Ethan's coffee knowledge reeled the viewers in. This was why he added the roasting business. People loved coffee, but they had no idea what was involved in making their favourite beverage. When they slowed down long enough and learned, it fascinated them. "Coffee is not exactly a serving of fruit," Ethan laughed. "I wish! Naturally processed beans have a far more fruity, earthy flavor than washed beans because the natural ones have been in contact with the cherry for longer."

Ethan lifted a premeasured amount of beans in his hands. He'd preheated the roaster, so all he had to do was pour the beans into the drum.

"What's the computer doing?" Addison pointed at the laptop connected to the roaster.

"It monitors the temperature and tracks the first and second crack." Ethan could almost see the wheels turning in Addison and Eli's mind. By the end of next week, they'd probably pitch some crazy upgrade to the program. The beans entered the browning phase, and a sweet, familiar aroma wrapped the room in a hug.

Kathryn's features eased into a dreamy and soft

expression. "You all can't smell this, but I assure you, it's divine."

The scent transported Ethan back home. When he was a kid, he'd sneak downstairs and find his dad at the kitchen table with his steaming mug and newspaper. The smell of coffee made Ethan feel safe, how he always felt with his dad, until the day he realized his career choice was such a disappointment.

"What are you doing now?" Kathryn drew him back to the present.

Ethan gestured to the water tank behind him. "Better water produces better coffee. I use a filtration system that guarantees a lower mineral content." He poured coffee into their tiny mugs. "This brew has light notes of ripe fruit and a creamy body."

Kathryn wrinkled her nose adorably as she sniffed it. "Aren't we going to use the beans you're roasting right now?"

"No, those have to sit for a while before I can use them. I prepared the ones for tasting last week." Ethan casually slipped his hand into his front pocket and clutched his mother's heirloom ring. As soon as Kathryn took her first sip, he was going to offer her the raw sugar and ask her to sweeten his coffee forever by marrying him.

Kathryn lifted the mug to her lips, pausing so Gloria could get the shot.

Ethan white-knuckled his grip on the sugar bowl.

But before she could sip, the bells over the door jingled.

Shoot. He must not have locked it after the guy left.

Tiff entered, and Kathryn fumbled. Coffee sloshed over the rim. She shot a panicked glance at the camera before dipping her head. Something was going on between Kathryn and Tiff, something Kathryn didn't want her viewing audience or her friends to see.

Ethan transferred the roasted beans to the cooling bin and turned it on. With his back to the camera, he regrouped. He wasn't about to share the most important moment of his life with a semi-famous troublemaker.

Before Tiff could speak, the blades in the cooling bin squawked like nails on a chalkboard. All eyes, camera included, swung back to the screaming machine. Eli and Addison hopped over the counter, knocking his phone to the floor.

"What's happening?"

Ethan could barely hear Kathryn over the scraping noise. He powered down the machine. Once the spinning arm stopped, he stuck his hands inside and felt around. He lifted out a pebble. "Stones."

Eli and Addison began picking through the beans, removing more and more stones.

"Who would do such a thing?" Meg rested a protective hand over her belly as if the sabotage against Ethan's bakery was a threat to her baby.

Tiff bumped a chair, and it scraped the floor. Everyone turned as she backed up. "Clearly this is a bad time. I'll try later." The bells over the door jingled as Tiff hurried out the door.

Ethan retrieved his phone.

Coffee, $5. Metal scrapings? Free.

Coffee and a show.

Kathryn's audience had seen his failed launch. Great.

"That's enough for today," Kathryn spoke to the camera. "Tune in tomorrow for the answer to our very own Coffee Shop Mystery, titled, Who Stoned the Coffee Beans? Who knows, maybe my next book will be a cozy whodunit."

Gloria lowered the camera, and the group collectively sighed.

"That could have gone better," Eli said dryly, still picking stones from the cooling bin.

"I can't believe we just livestreamed that." Ethan collapsed onto a chair.

Kathryn stayed quiet. Too quiet. The spunky girl wooing the masses had evaporated. "I'm sorry."

She said it so softly the words took a minute to register. He met her gaze with a frown. "For what? It's not your fault."

She bit her lip in the way she always did when she was nervous. "It all got livestreamed. Another failed event I'm covering."

Ethan connected her dots. Just like what happened in Grander. But they couldn't be related. A competitor wouldn't destroy his life's work for a voting edge.

"If that was the plan, it backfired." Meg scanned her

phone. "The comments are in your favor. Sure, there are a few cruel ones, but for the most part, people are hoping everyone is okay and wishing you well." Meg handed him the phone. "They even hashtagged themselves #Cozy-CoffeeSleuths and pledged to get to the bottom of it."

"Jump on the hashtag and ride the wave," Eli advised. "Let them figure out who did it for you."

Ethan's phone vibrated. He handed Meg her device back. "Hi, Mom."

Ethan expected her to launch into a million questions about the bakery, the stones, and what he was going to do, but she didn't.

"Our retirement plans have been pushed back. Your dad has one more job he needs to finish."

"K. Thanks for letting me know." Ethan didn't have the brain space to get into it right now. "Can I call you back later?"

"Sure."

They disconnected. His mom sounded off. He'd figure out why when he called back. Ethan ran his gaze over his damaged supplies. What was he going to do?

Addison poked around in the cooling bin, searching for stones as if a carnival game prize hung in the balance. "Did you have any trouble with the equipment?"

"None."

"Who else handled the beans?" Eli added a few more pebbles to the growing collection.

"Just me. The delivery guy left them at the back door because he got here about fifteen minutes early. He sent

46

pic and a text message confirming the delivery. I brought them inside as soon as I arrived."

"Maybe we should loop in Jackson?" Having a friend in the police department sometimes gilded their gingerbread. "If someone added stones to your delivery, they only had a fifteen-minute window. There could be video surveillance in the alley."

Maybe. But Ethan wasn't holding his breath.

Chapter Five

K athryn's online promotions sent a surge of new customers to The Muffin Man, forcing Kathryn and Gloria to take their coffee to a table near the back. Ethan only used paper cups when people ordered to-go, so they cradled ceramic mugs, dodging people and smiling as they went.

Kathryn caught a whisper of her name. Three girls huddled in the corner and not-so-subtly looked at their phones, her, then back to their phones. Great. She'd been recognized as *that Kathryn*. She cranked the wattage on her smile and hoped the dark circles under her eyes didn't show on any unauthorized recordings that hit the web.

She and Gloria snagged a table, and their white mugs clunked down, each one boasting a clever saying etched in black script. Kathryn added cream to her *Espresso yourself*, and Gloria lifted *Warning! I'm a caffeine addict* to her lips.

Kathryn's digestive tract coiled at the light-hearted use of the word *addict*.

Ambrosial hints of freshly baked goods and rich butter wafted from the kitchen. Meg hustled behind the counter, greeting customers and offering samples of Ethan's gourmet blends. Ethan hole-punched a coffee card and handed it back to a man. Based on the number of punches in the card, the man had been enjoying the coffee. Buzz, conversation, and clinking dishes played as a soft soundtrack.

The bustling scene released the pressure that had been steadily building in Kathryn's chest. Meg had been right about the coffee roaster incident. People were sympathetic toward Ethan's misfortune, just as sympathetic as they were toward her about her altercation with the vehicle and the mud puddle. Whoever was trying to discredit her was losing. Ethan's business held strong, and her popularity skyrocketed. In fact, both videos went viral, and they directed genuine coffee lovers who lived within the radius of Sycamore Hill to the Muffin Man— where she planned to livestream from the kitchen this afternoon with a famous internet foodie.

"Since we have a bit of time before we start," Gloria said, "I wanted to show you something." Gloria opened her laptop and spun it so Kathryn could see her screen. "I recorded some behind-the-scenes clips. I thought if I gathered enough, you might be able to turn the livestream off for a bit."

The knot in Kathryn's stomach that had been tightening since the contest began loosened. A day off sounded great. Impossible. Like magic. She dragged her finger over the trackpad and fast-forwarded through her friend's covert filming. Gloria had caught snapshots of her applying her film makeup, buying groceries, singing in church, laughing, and throwing popcorn at Ethan while the gang watched a movie. Gloria had captured beautiful B-reel film.

"When did you take this?" Kathryn pointed to the clip from church.

"I came in late because I was helping a fussy baby settle in the nursery. I saw you, and I thought it would be nice to show you just being you. You're so peaceful when you sing. But if filming in church crossed a line, you don't need to use it."

"Can I interest you ladies in a pastry?" Meg lowered a tray full of freshly baked goods and slices of apple pie with fragrant cloves and cinnamon spice. Under her breath, she added, "The girls at your nine o'clock are filming you."

Kathryn's mouth dried up, but she kept the smile on her face. "The pie, please."

Meg set a piece on the table in front of Kathryn. Gloria shook her head no, and Meg moved onto the girls, enticing them with the desserts and blocking their shot. "Recording someone without their permission might be legal, but posting it online can get you into a whole mess of trouble."

Kathryn tried not to smile as they ducked their heads and mumbled apologies.

"What do you think?" Gloria drew her attention back to the computer screen.

If she edited the clips right, she'd be able to offset the livestreaming with these bits and get a breather. "This is fabulous work."

Gloria ran her fingertip over the trackpad and clicked a few times. "I had a question."

Kathryn nodded and took a bite of the pie. Delicious.

"What's happening here?" Gloria played the now-famous video of Kathryn in Grander getting splashed. She paused it when Tiff turned the camera to herself and signed off for Kathryn.

Kathryn choked. She hacked apple pie chunks into her napkin and gulped scorching coffee to clear her throat. *Oh please, Lord, if anyone recorded me choking, strike their phone with a bolt of lightning.*

"How do you know her?" Gloria's mouth twisted on the word her. It was always *her* or *that girl*. Never Tiff.

Dabbing her mouth with the napkin, Kathryn cleared her throat. "I don't. Not really. I only know the parts of her she's shared with me." Shared in confidential AA meetings that Kathryn couldn't talk about, not even with Gloria.

"Come on, Kathryn."

"I can't say." Wouldn't even if she could. Because if she did, her secret would be out, too. The only way

Kathryn could meet Tiff at an AA meeting was if she was in attendance herself.

Gloria's jaw moved back and forth, but the movement didn't hide her scowl. "I hope you know what you're doing. She wasn't just my roommate; she was my best friend. And she threw me under the bus to save herself, collecting a nice paycheck to boot. She only got a fine and court-ordered rehab because she agreed to help the prosecution build their case against Emergence Pharmaceuticals."

This was it. This was her window. She should tell Gloria that she met Tiff in rehab, because she wasn't breaking confidentiality if Gloria already knew she went, but her tongue stuck to the roof of her mouth.

"Like rehab actually rehabilitates," Gloria snorted. "It's only a matter of time before she relapses. She only went because it was a condition on her get-out-of-jail-free card. Do you know how much damage she could have done to the women of Life House if she wasn't exposed? If that drug trial had started—"

Kathryn tuned out. *Like rehab actually rehabilitates.* It landed like a punch. *It's only a matter of time before she relapses.* That's what Gloria thought about addicts. Kathryn channelled her fake smile that wooed the masses online. She carefully kept her body language relaxed and open.

Gloria wasn't the only one familiar with rejection. Kathryn knew it so well that she once nearly killed herself trying to numb the pain. But this wasn't about her. Tiff was trying to do the right thing, and Kathryn had to help her work the steps of her sobriety.

Kathryn tried to moisten her lips, but all the saliva in her mouth had evaporated. "Forgiveness rarely feels deserved, and it is never easy." She reached for Gloria's hand. "But if you don't forgive, the bitterness will eat you alive."

Gloria turned away. A few minutes passed before she spoke again. "Forgiveness doesn't mean we trust someone who has proven to be untrustworthy. We are to be wise as serpents. It's in the Bible."

"And harmless as doves. That's the rest of that verse. Holding onto bitterness doesn't feel harmless."

Gloria flattened her lips. It wasn't a frown, but it wasn't a smile, either. "I'm trying, Kathryn. I really am."

"You ladies ready?"

Kathryn jumped at Ethan's interruption. She was so focused on Gloria, she hadn't noticed him standing beside the table.

Ethan's head swivelled from Kathryn to Gloria. "The food blogger arrived. He's in the kitchen."

Kathryn collected their dishes, and Gloria closed the computer. They stood.

"Have either of you seen a bakery key lying around? Addison and Eli lost one of theirs." Ethan chewed on his bottom lip.

"No, but we'll keep an eye out," Gloria promised.

They followed Ethan to the back. Last night, Ethan had set out premeasured ingredients and the small appliances they needed on the back prep counter. An up-and-coming food blogger from TasteBud Explosions was going to try the results of their short baking segment. They got the shot in one take, which was amazing. Kathryn channelled all her tension into charm, and within minutes, she had Mr. TasteBud in stitches.

She was ready to prematurely call the segment a victory when Mr. TasteBud lifted their scrumptious looking creation to his lips. He took a bite—a big one.

Gloria zoomed in for his reaction as all the wonderful gooey goodness slid down his throat.

Instead of smiling, he exploded in gags and spit into a napkin. There might have even been a bit of dry heaving, all live on internet TV.

"That's awful!" He furiously wiped his mouth. "It's loaded with salt." He downed an entire water bottle in one swig.

"I measured these myself." Ethan swiped a finger in the now empty sugar bowl and licked. His mouth puckered. "Salt."

Kathryn looked directly into the camera, still broadcasting. "Our coffee shop saboteur strikes again."

Chapter Six

E than looked at his watch for what must have been the tenth time in as many minutes. He peered through the window on the bakery door. Ben should be here. His friend never said what the urgency was, but Ethan figured he was writing some sort of article for the paper about the recent mysterious happenings at The Muffin Man.

His leg bounced. The last week had been a flurry of activity. Despite several setbacks, the promo Kathryn generated drew in a crowd. Everyone wanted to know who was targeting The Muffin Man, and ideas abounded that were crazier than the fake moon landing and flat earth theories. Ethan was supposed to open in an hour, and if the trend continued, he'd need every second to prepare. He tried telling Ben that, but Ben insisted they meet.

Today.

This morning.

Before opening.

Ethan looked at his watch.

He unlocked the bakery door and stared down the street. Through the foggy morning haze, two figures emerged.

Finally!

Ben hurried up the sidewalk with his wife, Emma. Ethan ushered them inside before locking the door again.

Ben didn't even say hello. He thrust a newspaper toward Ethan. "Did you see this?"

After motioning for them to take a seat at the small bistro table nearest to the kitchen, Ethan took the paper from Ben. Two coffees waited for them, along with a small pitcher filled with cream and a bowl of raw sugar packets. "I made you a coffee. It's a new blend I'm trying."

Ben pulled out a chair for Emma, and Ethan turned around the chair across from them and straddled it. He unfolded the paper.

Neither Ben nor Emma touched the coffee.

Pressure built in Ethan's chest as he processed the local headline. His gut heaved. *Local Bakery Brews Controversial Kopi-Luwak Coffee. Should Citizens Be Concerned?*

"You've got to be kidding." He'd only just recovered from the stone incident. Then the disastrous baking segment spoiled his publicity idea and his new plan to propose to Kathryn. After the food blogger had raved about his delicious treat, Ethan intended to drop to one knee and offer to be Kathryn's personal chef for life. But nothing about yesterday panned out the way he'd hoped.

He tightened his grip on the paper. And it never would, if the press had its way.

Ben made a face. "If I'd seen it, I would have killed it. I'm sorry."

A bolt of pain shot through Ethan's jaw, and he scrubbed a hand down his chin. "Someone has it out for my business."

Ben's nostrils flared. "That's what I was thinking."

"Do you think it's someone local?" Ethan tossed the paper on the table. He couldn't imagine any of his direct competitors stooping to this level, but the economy was tough, and desperate people did desperate things.

"I don't know, but I'm gonna look into it," Ben promised.

Ethan pushed his sleeves up and pulled at his collar. Everything suddenly felt tight. Too constricting. It made it hard to breathe. Whoever said there was no such thing as bad press was never accused of serving coffee made from pooped-out coffee cherries. Ethan's stomach flipped as another realization struck him. *It's Grander's paper.* "My dad's gonna see this."

"He won't believe it." Emma shook her head. She gave his dad too much credit. Except Dad had been watching him lately. He even followed The Muffin Man online. Maybe Dad was trying?

Ethan lurched to his feet. The chair skidded a few

inches. He paced a semi-circle around the table. "I can't control what anyone believes." He understood that logically, but that didn't help the churning in his gut. If Dad really was trying to connect, this would only give him another reason to criticize his career. Another reason to try and convince him to hang up his apron and pick up a nail gun like Dad always wanted. Except—Dad hadn't asked in a while. In fact, Ethan couldn't remember the last time Dad had asked him to consider a career change. Maybe there was something to Mom's claims, after all?

The oven beeped. Ethan trudged to the kitchen and removed a tray of muffins. He placed it on a counter already filled with dozens and dozens of cooling baked goods. The urgency to open had vanished.

"It's not true, is it?" Emma's cringe was unmistakeable, even from the kitchen. It sank what was left of his hope. Was that why his friends left their coffee untouched? If they had to ask, strangers would just run with the rumor. It was the ice cream topping on today's mud pie.

"Of course, it's not." He yanked off his oven mitts and chucked them on the counter.

A faint blush shaded Emma's cheeks, and he instantly felt guilty. It took a tremendous amount of self-control to not stomp back to the table, but he managed to rejoin them without throwing the tantrum brewing in his soul. He spun the chair so it faced them and slumped into it.

"Is it really made from partially digested coffee berries?"

Ethan blew out a sigh. "Yes. Kopi-Luwak comes from coffee cherries that are eaten and defecated." Ethan might as well say it. Everyone would be wondering about it. Thinking it. "But I don't serve it."

His attention drifted to the front window. The sun was rising and soon, the street would fill with shoppers. But he'd probably have more protestors than customers.

"Hey"—Ben reeled him back in—"I've seen this type of story before. The best thing you can do is be proactive. Show people that your business practices are ethical." Ben opened the paper to the full-page spread. It featured Kopi Luwak's popularity with high-end roasters and images of the poor Asian Palm Civets caged at unethical farms.

Ethan blinked, too stunned to respond. This smear took the cake. Or, more accurately, the muffins.

"The paper takes false reporting seriously, and since this is untrue"—Ben stabbed the article with his index finger—"whoever wrote it is going to be in big trouble. I'll push for a retraction."

"Thanks." But the damage was done. People couldn't unread a headline. It might be impossible to unscramble this omelette. Ethan dug his fingers into his hair, tangling them in the hairnet he forgot he wore. He tugged it off his head.

"You survived the other things. You'll survive this." Emma's promise sounded nice, but the fact she still hadn't sipped her coffee undermined her good intentions.

His cell phone rang, and the call display lit up his mom's name. Lately, she seemed to have a knack for phoning moments after a disaster. He sent her to voice-mail, only feeling the tiniest twinge of guilt. He didn't have the emotional bandwidth for his parents right now.

"My dad's always wanted me to take over his business. I've spent more money than I have to buy the roaster. Maybe it's time to hang up my apron."

The shrill of his cell cut him off.

His mom.

Again.

He might as well get it over with. "Hey, Mom."

"We'll go," Ben whispered. "I'll write the follow-up story, so you don't need to worry about the content. We'll get to the bottom of this."

Ethan nodded absentmindedly, followed them to the door, and locked it after they left.

"Dad's in the hospital," Mom blurted.

His chest seized.

In the background, Dad scolded her. "I told you not to call him."

If Dad was talking, he had to be okay. "What happened?"

Ethan tugged a paper napkin from the dispenser and wiped the back of his neck. He might feel conflicted about his relationship with his dad, but he wasn't ready to say good-bye to him.

"He fell off a ladder on a job."

"Dad needs to stop doing this kind of work." He was

getting too old to shinny up ladders and walk across rooftops, but no matter how much he encouraged his father to retire, Dad pushed back. Clearly, Ethan's hope that their rental property in the north was the start of a retirement plan was premature.

"Shannon," his dad warned.

"Why was Dad on the ladder? Why wasn't Joel up there instead?" Dad's foreman was supposed to do the roof work so Dad could stay on the ground.

"Joel and Shelley had a wedding today, and we needed to finish the job."

"The job can wait."

"We need the payment, and your dad can't bill the customer until the job is done."

"Are you having money problems?" Had his parents stretched themselves too thinly buying the rental?

"Our too good to be true deal was too good to be true," Mom blurted.

"Let me talk to him." His father didn't sound injured. At least not physically. There was some muffled shuffling, and then Dad took the phone. "It was a real estate scam. I'm trying to get our money back, but until I do, I have to take a few more jobs."

Ethan stretched the skin between his eyebrows with his thumb and index finger. His dad couldn't stop working. "Why didn't you tell me?"

His gruff father wheezed, and the formidable man sounded surprisingly vulnerable. "I was embarrassed.

What kind of man loses his life's savings at this stage of the game?"

"How long until you get it back?"

Pause.

"Dad?"

Another shuffling sound and muffled words, then Mom was back on the phone. "We tried to sell it right away, but—it's complicated."

He knew all about complicated.

"We found a company that promised to resell our share. They required an upfront fee."

Ethan's stomach pitched again. That sounded like a refund and recovery scammer.

"We never heard from them after paying. Now we're getting calls from other people, and for another fee, they promise to get our money back."

"Don't pay anything!" His parents were on a sucker list, which meant every cheater in the province was about to descend.

Silence.

"You already did, didn't you?" The bakery door rattled against the deadbolt. Ethan held the phone with one hand and peeked through the blinds. Kathryn.

"We didn't know—" Mom cut off. More muffled sounds in the background. When she spoke again, her forced cheeriness made his eyes gummy. "It's almost time for you to open. We can chat later."

"I'll come as soon as I can." He swallowed, and a painful lump moved down his throat. He rubbed the butt of his palm in circles on his chest. Even his lungs hurt.

"I know you will." They disconnected.

Ethan opened the door, and Kathryn practically fell inside. Her white face and trembling lips heaped more weight on him. He struggled to breathe. *Lord, I don't know how much more I can take.*

"I don't know how it happened," she prattled. Kathryn never prattled. "But someone posted a picture of me drinking coffee here and said fans had no business supporting a woman that thumbed her nose at animal rights. A gourmet cup of coffee wasn't worth caging Asian Palm Civets. It linked to an awful article—"

Ethan crushed her against his chest. "I know. Ben and Emma were already here. It's not your fault. A freelancer sent the story to Grander."

Kathryn mumbled into his shoulder. "If only I wasn't in this stupid contest."

"It's not your fault."

"How can you say that? I'm the target. You're collateral damage."

Ethan didn't like the way she owned it. This contest had wound her tighter than a coiled whisk. No, that wasn't quite right. She started acting like she was a few eggs short of a dozen when Tiff arrived, and the few eggs she had were cracked.

Kathryn pulled away from him and tilted her head back so she could look into his eyes. "If I hadn't been filming here or working on a coffee book, none of this would have happened."

Ethan shook his head. "If you hadn't been filming here, I wouldn't have had my best week since adding the roaster."

Her eyes widened. "Really?"

He nodded. "The stones drummed up sympathy for me. This will turn out to be good as well. You'll see." Ethan didn't feel half as confident as he pretended, but he was clinging to God's promise to use all things for good in the lives of his children. Even if God might define good differently than he did.

Kathryn bit down on the corner of her lower lip in the way she often did when she was thinking. "What if I used my social media fan base to get out ahead of any more negative stories?"

"How?"

"Blogs, videos with customer testimonials, public appearances—anything that might help build trust in your brand again and reassure customers that there is no truth to any of this nonsense. We could create a certification label for your coffee that guarantees it is ethically sourced."

"If I provided a certificate guaranteeing my coffee's ethical origins, customers would know they can trust that it's not from the kinds of places that mistreat animals." He liked this. He liked it a lot.

Ideas spilled from Kathryn. "You should create a blog post or video apart from me, explaining why you don't source Kopi Luwak beans. I'll cross post it on all my social media feeds, and ask my followers open-ended questions to get a dialogue flowing."

"We could expand it. Talk about why I don't use any unethical products."

"It might also be helpful for you to highlight the steps you take when sourcing fair trade coffee beans so customers can have full confidence in the quality of your product. You know, like you did on our coffee tour."

Ethan smiled. It was a great idea. He and Kathryn would tackle this problem head on. They'd do it together because they'd always been better together, like a perfect salty and sweet combination. His gaze flicked to the cupboard where he'd stashed the engagement ring. Maybe he didn't need to wait for the perfect moment. Maybe the moment was now?

Kathryn turned into his arms. "I believe in you." Her warm breath sent a shiver down his back. "We can do this."

No, not now. It was nearly time to open, and he didn't want to propose and have to shove her out the door. Besides, since the cooking disaster, he'd reconsidered his plans. He wasn't sure he wanted to share the most important decision of their lives with customers or fans. He'd keep the ring on him and wait for the perfect moment and just ask. That was the new plan.

Ethan pressed his lips to Kathryn's forehead and framed his strategy to earn back the trust of his customers. He'd create content for the bakery's social media platforms and send an email campaign with customer testimonials and positive stories about his business. He'd turn this ship around. And if Kathryn worked her magic behind the scenes by helping him spread the word, they both might get everything they wanted.

His watch vibrated on his wrist. Eight o'clock. With one arm around Kathryn, he unlocked the deadbolt to The Muffin Man. There wasn't a customer in sight.

Chapter Seven

The phone trembled in Kathryn's hand. It vibrated with another notification. Someone had commented on or liked the post. Not her post. Not the fun reel she'd put up earlier this morning. The action wasn't happening on Ethan's feed either. He'd uploaded a video in response to the smear article. Kathryn commented on it, sharing his outrage over the false claims. Both of those threads were suspiciously quiet. She'd checked.

Then double-checked.

The reel gaining traction originated with some internet troll that tagged Kathryn in a montage of photographs from her university days. Not just any pictures of her, but the intoxicated, hard-partying her. The her she hadn't been for years and, with the Lord's help, would never be again. Swiping with her thumb, she flipped through the images. Revulsion shot up her throat. The snapshots hijacked her brain and transported her into the past.

Her mouth watered at the sight of a bottle against her lips. It was like someone had rewired her pleasure circuits in a blink. She could almost feel the cool, smooth glass. The pressure of the bottle. The burn in her throat. She ground her teeth. Just because her body reacted with a longing she'd hoped she'd killed years ago didn't mean she had to give into the urge to indulge.

She wouldn't indulge. Not even mentally.

She forced herself to detach. To think logically. To investigate. The poster had to have dug deep into her history to get his hands on these pictures. That meant taking her down wasn't an impulsive decision. He'd invested in her. Looked for the people willing to share. This was premeditated sabotage, and if it came from the same person targeting Ethan, it was proof she'd pulled the bakery into her damaged orbit.

She was the rat in Ethan's kitchen.

Her device dinged again. Another comment.

The knots in her stomach tightened. The brutal thread of responses attached to the post was even more humiliating than the photos. Her phone kept chiming as the world interpreted what they saw. She turned the device face down on the table and gagged on the sob rising in her throat.

She lurched to the nearest window and pulled the cord for the blinds, cutting off the sunlight. In the living room, she tugged her fabric curtain panels closed, dropped onto the sofa, and cradled her pounding head. She had worked too hard for it to end like this. Yet, her dirty laundry flapped in the online breeze for everyone to see.

To comment on.

There were too many opinions about the stability of recovering addicts.

She lunged to the kitchen and vomited in the garbage can. After rinsing her mouth, she dragged a sleeve across her lips and slid to the floor. She should have never agreed to let her name stand on the contest. Her pride did this. Her misguided need to be chosen might undo all her progress in life. Her chest heaved even as her breaths shallowed. The room swayed. She forced her head between her knees and inhaled deeply. It took a few seconds for her heart to slow and her vision to clear. As soon as it did, she snagged her phone off the table and scrolled. It was like driving past a car wreck. She knew she shouldn't look, but she couldn't help it. Her gut flipped again.

Most of the comments were negative. The web thrived on a good scandal, and the trolls loved nothing better than shaming a person who claimed to love Jesus. It didn't matter if the story was true. All that mattered was the juice oozing from the details.

The smattering of kind comments that contained understanding were not loud enough to turn down the negative. Anything good was buried in cynicism within seconds of appearing.

Ding.

Fair or not, the secret was out. Kathryn was a drunk. Is a drunk. According to rehab will always be a drunk. At best, she could strive to live her life publicly as a sober alcoholic that never forgot sobriety was achieved and maintained one day at a time.

Ding.

She pushed her fingertips into her forehead and stretched the skin. The tightness felt good. Like a mini endorphin release. Was it so bad they knew?

Maybe not, except that her competition was using it as a reason people shouldn't vote for her. As a reason for people to boycott The Muffin Man.

The headlines taunted.

Small town girl hides big time secret.

Who is the real Kathryn Withers?

Not role model material.

And when Ethan saw it, he'd never look at her the same way again.

Tiff's name popped up on her phone screen. *Are you okay?*

Yeah.

Do you need company?

Code for, are you tempted to drink? Do you need a chaperone? Do you have access to booze?

No.

I'm here if you change your mind.

Kathryn gave it a thumbs up. She didn't believe Tiff was involved even if her modus operandi was public humiliation. Tiff was the only one who reached out. Fresh pressure climbed up her throat. Where were her friends? Why weren't they texting? Had Ethan seen it yet?

Her doorbell rang.

Kathryn pushed to her feet and padded to the door. She lifted onto her toes to peek through the peephole.

Gloria. Owen stood just behind her.

Kathryn melted a little. Gloria didn't call because she came. Kathryn pressed her forehead against the door. *Lord, I know I asked where they were, but I'm not sure I'm ready.*

"I can see your shadow," Gloria said. "Please, let us in."

Kathryn opened the door. She wasn't sure what she expected, but whatever it was, it wasn't what happened. Gloria flung her arms around her and hugged her tightly.

Kathryn stumbled back a few steps, but Gloria held firm. Hope bubbled up from that deep place inside that had been afraid her friends wouldn't stand by her.

Of course, Gloria came.

Owen closed the door behind them.

After what felt like forever, Gloria finally released her. "I saw the awful things they wrote. And those pictures! They have to be photoshopped. Why would someone do that?"

Kathryn's mouth dried up. She tried to dampen her lips, but couldn't. She jerked her gaze to Owen, who nodded. He'd already connected the dots Gloria refused to consider.

Kathryn squared her shoulders. It was time. She settled her eyes on Gloria. "They did it because it's true."

Gloria's mouth slackened. In fact, the intensity in her entire posture diminished. She stared with such a mix of disbelief and confusion that Owen slipped an arm around her. But to her credit, she stayed calm.

"Why don't we sit down," Owen suggested.

Kathryn's apartment was a modest one bedroom. The living room held a sofa and one occasional chair. Kathryn took the chair.

"Can you explain it to us?" Owen's question held no judgment and his posture no rigidity. Owen was just Owen, her friend and her pastor.

Kathryn tucked a strand of hair behind her ear and sucked in a breath. She held it a moment, waiting for the thickness in it to subside. She might as well get used to answering questions. She'd be telling her story a lot over the next few days.

Here I go, Lord. For better or worse.

Her cheeks tingled hotly. "I'm a sober alcoholic. I've been sober for years now, but my story is not something I've ever shared with anyone except my sponsor and the others in recovery meetings."

"When did it start?"

"High school." Kathryn averted her eyes. She'd told her story so many times in so many church basements that it rolled from her lips as naturally as breathing. But reactions didn't matter as much in those settings. This was different. This was with people she cared about.

"I was at a party when someone twisted off the top of a beer and handed it to me. I drank it to fit in. I didn't even like it, but it took the edge off."

"The edge of what?" Gloria interjected. Fair question.

She shrugged. "High expectations. Teachers, parents, my friends. Everyone thought they knew who I should be, but no one ever asked me what I wanted. Eventually, I liked how I felt when I drank even if I didn't like the taste."

"High school." Gloria echoed, stuck on the timeline. Her brow furrowed. "I was in high school with you. How come I didn't know this?"

"I was a few years ahead of you. We ran in different circles. And really, it didn't become an issue until university. Until then, I was a social drinker."

Gloria reached across the tiny coffee table separating them. She extended her hand and waited.

Kathryn's gaze dropped to the offering. She lifted her hand slowly. Unsure.

Gloria clasped it and squeezed. "I feel like I should have been there for you."

Kathryn swallowed. Letting Gloria work through misplaced guilt was part of the process. But there was more. What was the saying? In for a penny, in for a pound? She tugged her hand free and folded it in her lap. "Everyone seemed to juggle expectations better than me.

I turned to booze more and more. By the time I got to university, I was depending on it just to make it through the day. When I came to class with it on my breath, my roommate gave me an ultimatum—tell someone I had a problem or she would. My parents put me in rehab, and I cleaned up and graduated only a half year after my friends."

"Why didn't you tell us?"

"Have *you* told everyone the things in your past that you are the most ashamed about?" Kathryn snapped.

Gloria grunted. "I didn't need to. The minute I returned to town, the local gossip chain did it for me."

"And you hated it," Kathryn said. Gloria might know what it was like to crave acceptance from people unwilling to look past your faults, but their experiences were like comparing apples and oranges. Sure, both were fruit, but they were fundamentally different at their core. Gloria's scandal was based on misunderstandings. Kathryn deserved what she got. Her gaze fell to her hands on her lap. When would her debt be paid? When would she stop reaping the consequence of her choices? She tucked her hands under her thighs to stop her fidgeting.

Owen gently cut in. "Where have you been attending meetings?"

Of course, Owen knew she didn't attend local meetings because they were held in the church basement.

"Grander. Not as many people know me there."

"Is that where you met Tiff?" Gloria finally pieced

the puzzle together. It was no secret that Tiff blamed addiction for her questionable decisions.

"Yes."

"We're here for you, Kathryn. Whatever you need. This," Owen pointed at the phone, still humming with comments, "is not who you are."

She snorted. Wasn't it? She'd hid her real self from her best friends. When Tiff needed her, she backed away. Alcoholics perpetually put themselves first, sacrificing others on the altar of their desire. She pulled her knees into her chest and made herself as small as possible. It was the story of her life, but she desperately wanted this telling to have a different ending. "It doesn't matter. It's who they think I am. That'll be enough for the publisher to pull the book deal. Enough to tank my show."

She was going to lose it all.

"Look at me." Owen waited until she did. "You are a new creation in Christ. And when Jesus took your sins, he also gave you His holiness. You were saved, are saved, will be saved by a Savior who was, is, and is to come. This"—he pointed at the phone—"doesn't define you." He pointed up. "He does."

Were saved, are saved, will be saved. Was an addict, is an addict, will always be an addict. She looked away. She felt stupid. How could something so massive catch her off guard? It was just like addiction. It happened when a person wasn't looking, and by the time they realized the risk, it was done.

The phone hummed again, and Gloria picked it up. "Your trolls are really throwing gasoline on this fire."

"That's because alcohol addiction is still heavily stigmatized," Owen said. "People think they can't trust or respect someone who has ever struggled with substance abuse."

Gloria plucked her bottom lip. "Do you think Tiff tipped them off?"

All the warmth growing in Kathryn's chest froze. "That's a perfect example of what Owen just said. You don't trust Tiff. Even though she has tried to explain what she did was because of her addiction. Even though she is different now, has tried to make amends—"

"—make excuses."

"We're not here to argue about Tiff," Owen cut in. "We're here for you, Kathryn. And you're the same person you were yesterday, only now you've got this public victory under your belt."

Kathryn shifted her gaze from Gloria to Owen and then back to Gloria.

"That's something worth celebrating," Gloria said softly. Almost apologetically.

"And maybe even something worth posting about online," Owen added.

Kathryn froze. "Posting?"

"Take control of the narrative. Sobriety isn't something to be ashamed of; it's a hard-won victory in your life that doesn't disqualify you from God's family. It's part of what God used to draw you *into* the family. So, stand up. Own your past. Share your story. Refuse to worry about what people might think of you or how they might judge you because it's about more than you. It's about what God has done in you, and what He can do for others if they are willing to trust Him."

Kathryn didn't answer. She couldn't. It was more complicated than Owen knew. She didn't want to be the poster girl for sobriety. She didn't build a public life around the most shameful choices she'd made. She built a public life to . . . to . . .

Why did she build a public life?

To prove to herself she was worthy of admiration? To show all those people who rejected her that she'd made it? What was she trying to prove? Who was she trying to prove it to? She glanced at her phone still in Gloria's hand. Why hadn't Ethan reached out? Why wasn't he the one knocking on her door?

The phone buzzed. Kathryn extended her hand palm up, and Gloria handed the device over. Kathryn didn't bother reading the message. She just powered it down. If Ethan rejected her because of this, she wouldn't survive.

Chapter Eight

I t was hours before sunrise when Ethan stabbed his key into The Muffin Man's deadbolt. Yesterday had been a disaster. The longest twenty-four hours of his life. The majority of the customers through his door had used the hashtag #CozyCoffeeSleuths, and without ordering a single item, they spent the day posting online and peppering him with questions about coffee and Kopi-Luwak and health code violations. To add insult to injury, he learned about Kathryn's crisis second-hand. While trying to keep up with the comments on his public response, someone mentioned Kathryn's addiction, and it sent him down a rabbit hole.

The cherry on that sundae was a trip to the hospital to see his dad and look over the real estate paperwork his parents signed. Then, he grieved with them over what it all meant. They could lose everything. The only good thing to come from it was when Dad had said how he should have done his research like Ethan did before investing in coffee. It was almost a compliment. Ethan tried reaching out to Kathryn to loop her in regarding his parents, but it went straight to voice mail. He sent off several text messages telling her that he wished he could be with her. He anticipated a typical sassy comeback or at least a compassionate word for his folks, but he got nothing but crickets.

Crickets from her, nosiness from others.

He'd been just about to ask Jackson to do a welfare check when Owen connected. Kathryn was fine. She'd turned off her phone. She didn't want to talk.

After putting out his own fires, he got it. At least he tried to get it. Talking about it while you were dealing with it was overwhelming. Owen encouraged him to take care of his parents, address the business issues, and keep them updated. Owen assured him that he and Gloria would stay with Kathryn, and they'd let her know why Ethan wasn't there.

Owen managed the crisis, not Ethan. Gloria comforted Kathryn, not him. If anyone should be with Kathryn, it was him, but he was the one she pushed away, and for the life of him, he couldn't figure out why. If they had any hope of having the future that he wanted them to have, they needed to be a couple. They needed to be there for each other. That meant Kathryn should have been at the hospital with him, but she wasn't. He should be at her place right now, but he wasn't. And the implications of those facts made his heart hurt.

Ethan flipped the bakery lights and locked the door behind him as a small crash sounded in the backroom.

"Eli? Addison?" He moved toward the noise. Eli and Addison had eventually located the lost bakery key. Or, to be more accurate, a customer had found it stuck behind the napkin dispenser and turned it in. Sometimes he could hear the guys in their shared hallway, but hardly ever at five o'clock in the morning.

Another rustle. This time closer.

Ethan's heart thumped. He slowed to a crawl, advancing toward the kitchen flicking on lights as he went. As he neared the coffee roaster, a shadow leapt over the counter and shoved him aside.

Ethan fumbled for the nearest barstool, toppling it on his way down. His head bounced off the vinyl flooring. Rebounding quickly wasn't fast enough. By the time his eyeballs stopped vibrating in his skull, the shadow had disappeared out the back door.

Ethan rubbed the back of his head, and his hand came back sticky. He swayed, catching himself against the counter and smearing blood along the edge. The police. He had to call Jackson.

Stuffing his hand in to his pocket, he retrieved his phone, fumbling through his contacts to find his friend's number.

"I'll be right there," Jackson promised. "I'll call Emma."

Ethan sank to the ground. *What else, Lord? Hasn't it been enough?*

. . .

"Can you stop by the shop? Someone broke into the bakery." Ethan massaged his pounding head. At least Kathryn finally answered his call. A part of him had expected her to send him to voicemail.

"Are you okay?" Kathryn's voice wobbled.

Ethan dragged a hand through his hair, brushed against the bruised spot, and winced. No, everything wasn't okay. Not for a million reasons. But he couldn't get into any of that. Not yet. She might not come. He deflected. "Everyone's here except you and Gloria."

"Gloria's with me. She spent the night."

"Eli and Addison are going to try to fix the busted computer, but if I can't get the roasting program running, it'll be out of commission indefinitely."

"We'll be there as soon as we can."

"See you soon." Ethan rubbed his forehead. The strong prescription Emma had filled for him hardly took the edge off. His wound didn't need stitches, thank the Lord, but it was ridiculously tender.

He decided to close the bakery for the day and posted a sign on the door that apologized for the disruption. He updated his social media accounts, and theorists pounced, surmising he couldn't take the scrutiny on his brewing practices. If he couldn't take the heat, they'd said, he should get out of the kitchen. Ethan didn't dignify the comments with a response. He wasn't even sure he cared anymore.

While online, he'd checked Kathryn's web station. Sycamore Hill at Sunrise ran a repeat.

"She's on her way." Ethan turned to his friends seated around the largest table in his dining area. Eli and Meg, Jackson and Kim, Ben and Emma, and Owen were here. Kathryn had withdrawn from them all, and the girls insisted they do something to show her their unwavering support. Ethan's break-in provided the perfect opportunity.

Ethan wasn't sure. It gave off *intervention vibes*, and Kathryn didn't need one. Owen insisted she was managing fine, but the girls were adamant. Ethan rubbed his midsection. His gut roiled more than the time he'd used outdated milk in a muffin recipe.

Within fifteen minutes, the bell above the door tinkled. Kathryn hurried inside, her face drawn into a worried frown as she scanned the room for Ethan.

Gloria followed.

Kathryn shrugged out of her light jacket and hung it on the hook by the door. "What's the plan?"

He moved toward her, but before he could speak, her eyes widened. All the color drained from her face. Her hand trembled as she gently brushed the backs of her fingertips against his cheek. "You're hurt."

He covered her hand with his, turning into her palm. "You're hurt, too."

She jerked her hand free and stepped back.

"Please sit." Meg motioned to a chair.

Kathryn didn't move, so Ethan nudged her toward

the empty chair beside Kim. Kathryn narrowed her eyes but obediently sat down. "What's going on?"

Kim scooped up Kathryn's hand and squeezed it briefly before letting go. "We want you to know that we're here for you."

Kathryn snapped her gaze to Ethan's. Confusion colored her face.

"Someone broke into the shop." He backpedaled. "That's why everyone came here." He knew their focus on Kathryn was a bad idea.

"He called me to report it," Jackson said. "I brought Emma to treat him, and Kim tagged along."

"Where's Oliver?"

"My parents are in town," Kim answered.

"I showed up for work," Meg said. "That's how I heard about it."

"And we were in the office upstairs." Eli answered for him and Addison.

"After I made the report," Jackson said, "we started talking about you."

"Me?" Kathryn echoed. She blinked rapidly and clenched her fists in her lap. "He's been hurt. Someone broke into his business, probably the same someone who has been trying to sabotage him for days, and you talked about me?"

Ethan scooted a chair closer to Kathryn and sat in front of her. "We've seen the online comments. We love you, and we want to be here for you. Tell us how."

Kathryn's phone rang. The muffled sound from

inside her purse crackled in the hostile air. Kathryn pushed to her feet, walked a few steps away, and turned her back on the group. "Hello?"

Ethan skimmed his gaze over each of his friends. This wasn't how it was supposed to go, and they looked just as flustered as he felt. Kathryn's clipped responses to whomever was on the other side of her call only cranked the tension dial in the room.

Kathryn disconnected, but she didn't turn to face them.

"What's wrong?"

Nothing.

His chair scraped against the floor as he stood. He gently laid his hand against her shoulder, and she spun. The flash in her eyes stole his breath.

"The publisher cancelled the coffee book deal. I've had too much bad press. But you all know about my bad press. It's why we're here, isn't it?"

Her reaction sent equal shots of defensiveness and thrill through him. He hadn't seen Kathryn so passionate, so human in years. This was the woman behind the mask. The woman he'd caught glimpses of, the one he remembered from camp but had since been hiding behind layers of film makeup. This was the Kathryn he fell in love with, and she wasn't the people-pleasing, self-deprecating public pushover she'd somehow morphed into over the years. And she was just getting started.

"You want to know why I haven't opened up? This is why. Here." She swept her arm across her body in a massive gesture. "I haven't changed. I'm still the same person I was last week and the week before that. The only thing that is different is that you all know I attend recovery meetings." She dragged her gaze over each one of them. "Ethan is the one in crisis, but you're all here to talk about my resolved past. None of this"—she gestured with both hands now, swirling them in front of her body as if she was waxing the floor—"is necessary. And it is exactly why I never told anyone."

Ethan didn't know whether to correct her or cheer. He went with correction. "They were here for me. They came right away."

She gave him a bitter smile. "But you didn't call me. Not until after."

And there it was. The reason for her pain. He could say it was because she shut him out yesterday. He could blame it on a lot of things. They had equal amounts of skin in this crime, but now wasn't the time to divide responsibility. He'd been so consumed with how her withdrawal yesterday had hurt him that he'd turned around and hurt her.

Kathryn strode to the coat hooks and snatched her jacket from the rack.

Ethan trailed her. "I should have come over yesterday. I should have insisted you let me. Then, I could have told you about my dad. You'd have been my first call today—"

"What about your dad?" Her knuckles whitened where they clutched her jacket.

Ethan briefly recapped his parents' ordeal, starting

with the work accident and ending with bleak financial outlook.

"Let me look into it," Jackson interjected. "Crimes targeting seniors are on the rise, and I can pass this along to the cop heading up the division in Grander. Maybe they've heard of the scheme."

"Wait." Kathryn opened her photos on her phone. "I saw them in Grander. I have a picture of the guy who sold them the property. He was at the diner with your parents the day I was there." She found the image and held it up for Jackson and Ethan to see the image.

Jackson squinted. "Can you send me that? I think this is the guy the division has been watching. I'll forward it to him to confirm."

She tapped a few buttons. "Done." Kathryn shrugged into her coat and looked at Ethan. "I still need to go." But she said it gentler. Less angry. And she didn't move away when Ethan swayed close enough that his lips brushed against her hair.

"I'm sorry."

She lifted her face. Her wet eyes and rosy round spots high on her cheeks compounded his guilt.

"You can't fix this for me, Ethan." Her voice cracked. "You can't fix me. I need time to figure things out. Time to decide on my next steps."

Rejection sliced through him.

"I'm sorry." She slipped out the door without a kiss goodbye.

"We shouldn't have done it this way." Emma paced.

"I should have called her into the office and spoken with her alone."

"We shouldn't have done it at all," Ethan corrected her. "We should have trusted that Kathryn is a responsible woman who would have reached out if she needed us." Another awkward silence descended, but Ethan didn't feel the need to smooth this one over.

"I'd better file the report on your break-in," Jackson said.

"If I can take the computer, I might be able to create a patch that allows the program to run despite the trouble." Eli stood up as well.

"Go ahead." Ethan didn't care about his program anymore. His mind went with Kathryn.

The girls launched into a discussion. They proposed different strategies, such as creating an accountability system with one of them sending reminders if Kathryn started slipping back into unhealthy habits, creating goals that would keep her motivated and feeling successful.

Ethan didn't engage. They were treating her as if she had relapsed. She deserved better from them. From him. He felt desperate to make things right but wasn't sure that was even possible.

Chapter Nine

Kathryn turned off the main road and onto a side street. She rode with Gloria to the bakery, but now she wished she'd driven herself. The park was to her right, a school to her left, and her apartment a few more blocks away. She stomped instead of walked, not even aware of the force with which her feet hit the pavement until her shins began to ache. She slowed her pace, but her racing heart refused to decelerate.

There were a few people on park benches. A handful of cars drove by, and the schoolyard was empty. The morning sun hid behind the clouds and the grey pallor covering the neighbourhood matched her blackened mood. She tucked her hands into her pockets, kept her head down, and avoided eye contact, ignoring the weighty threats of the continually darkening sky. She needed to get home before someone recognized her, and the morning commuters would tumble from their houses any minute.

Shadows played peek-a-boo with the trees and shrubbery, but the shade didn't scare her. She'd survived worse darkness than a mid-summer morning storm, and she'd survive this.

Just breathe.

She inhaled the sweet, pungent, pre-gale aroma.

Listen.

The breeze intensified and rustled the branches. Leaves sanded against each other in a crispy spring symphony. Nature came alive with anticipation.

Feel.

Trepidation reverberated in her soul, increasing the pressure in her chest. But she was used to this. Unease. Indecision. Wanting to belong but learning you didn't quite fit. She was different, the girl not quite like the others. The familiarity of it was strangely comforting. Rejection felt safe. Recognizable. Like waters she could navigate because she had been swimming them her entire life. Even if the winds stirred into a funnel, ripped branches from the trees, and huffed and puffed their threats of violence, she was safe from the most dangerous threats. No one could hurt her if she didn't let them in.

Kathryn hitched her shoulders until the collar of her jacket covered her ears. She'd been sober for years. She'd made it through worse days without a drink, and she'd make it through today. It didn't matter that her fans had turned on her. It didn't matter that she'd lost the book deal. It didn't even matter that her friends thought she was vulnerable. She knew who she was, and that was enough.

But if it was enough, why did she devote her life to presenting a perfect Kathryn? Why did she set herself up to need the approval of others to succeed? Why wasn't what God said about her enough? *Was saved, is saved, will be saved* was far more powerful than *was an addict, is an addict, will always be an addict.*

A teardrop slid down her cheek, and she swiped it with the back of her hand. What went down at The Muffin Man felt like the intervention her university friends once staged. Her ego couldn't take it, wriggling and writhing like bolts of energy seeking ground. Her friends had good intentions, but their sincere concern landed on her already-wounded pride. Truth was catching up with her, and she couldn't outrun it anymore. *Lord, forgive me.* If she could just get to her apartment. Get inside before the sky opened and everything she'd been fighting to keep contained poured from the heavens.

The clouds moved and shrouded the earth under a blanket. Instantly, the neighborhood darkened. It was as if the forecasted storm heard her goal and received it as a personal challenge to beat. Sheet lightening flashed a megawatt grin, but the following thunder never came. The sense of urgency lifted. The heavens could play with the dimmer switch all it wanted, and the clouds could keep blowing smoke, but until the storm gave a thunderous war cry, it remained miles away.

"Kathryn?"

She jumped. She could just make out the figure of a person sitting on the park bench. A woman, judging from her shape, with a grip on a bottle wrapped in a plain brown paper bag that rested on the bench beside her.

"It's Tiff." The shadow sniffed and dragged a forearm across her face. A bright flash briefly illuminated Tiff's face; this time followed by a faint rumble in the distance. The storm inched closer.

"Are you okay?" Kathryn perched on the bench beside Tiff, the bottle of alcohol sandwiched between them. Now she was closer she could see her blotchy skin and puffy eyes. But the puffy eyes were clear, thank God.

Tiff's eyes dropped to the unopened booze and lingered. After a few quiet seconds she lifted them back to Kathryn's. "No."

"Then I'll sit with you until you are." Kathryn leaned back on the bench and stuffed her hands into her pockets. The wind picked up, snatching tendrils of her hair and stretching them out. Kathryn couldn't solve Tiff's addiction, but a powerful God could use her presence. Tiff didn't need Kathryn to say anything. Kathryn didn't need to pry. She just needed to stay.

Staying affirmed the gravity of this moment. Kathryn's gift was proximity. She was here, and she would not leave. Not even if the heavens opened and pounded their souls.

Kathryn patterned her response after the One perfect at the ministry of presence. Not just being passively present but being actively present. Compassion always moved Jesus to act. She moved the bottle from between them on the bench to her other side. She'd do whatever it took to stop a fellow sinner from taking a drink or popping a pill, and she'd do so while displaying the gentleness of her Savior.

If she could fill this gap for someone else, why did she bristle when her friends tried to fill it for her? She pushed her arrogance aside.

They sat quietly. The temperature dipped with each minute. Without a word being exchanged, Kathryn gave Tiff's hand a gentle squeeze. The warmth radiating from Tiff filled some of the emptiness inside Kathryn. They sat for what felt like an eternity.

Finally, Tiff broke the silence. "I didn't think it would be this hard."

"Gloria and Kim still won't hear you out?"

The first fat drops began to fall. "I made a counselling appointment with Kim, so I was able to speak with her."

"Sneaky." Kathryn leaned and bumped Tiff's shoulder with hers. She didn't know whether to be impressed or not.

A tiny smile broke Tiff's hard features. She tipped her head back and closed her eyes. The rain landed sporadically. One drop on the shoulder wicked away by the fabric of her shirt. Another on her head. A cold pellet landed on Kathryn's cheek and dripped like a tear. She wiped it away.

"After about twenty minutes," Tiff said, "Kim finally relaxed and engaged. We'll never be friends, and she'll never trust me, but she forgave me."

A bit of the weight compressing Kathryn's lungs lifted. She didn't squeeze Tiff's hand or even tug up her hood. The moment felt too fragile to move. "So why the purchase?" She lifted her chin toward the bottle.

Tiff's mouth twitched. "I went straight to Gloria's after meeting Kim. Well, straight to her parents. I apologized to them first."

"And?"

"And they heard me out. They said all the right things, but I didn't feel forgiven."

"Forgiveness is a decision," Kathryn said. "If they said they forgave you, believe them. Their feelings will come as they live out the reality of having forgiven." Kathryn hadn't known the Sycamores to be anything except honest and sincere. "Take today's victory. I hear that two people forgave you. That's a massive win."

"Maybe."

"So why the bottle?" she pressed.

"I couldn't reach Gloria, and it suddenly felt impossible to try."

"That might be my fault." Kathryn wasn't surprised Gloria refused to take Tiff's call. Her friend was still deeply hurt by Tiff's betrayal. But the real reason for Gloria's rejection was simpler than Tiff knew. "Gloria was with me. I lost the book deal. My fan base has tanked. And my friends just held an intervention of sorts."

Tiff's eyes snapped to Kathryn's. "Are you drinking again?"

"No. But everyone just found out about my past. They're working through the discovery."

"How did that make you feel?"

She shrugged and averted her eyes. "Like I let everyone down. Like I'm the same screw-up that nearly threw away my life." Kathryn picked up the paper bag and pulled out the bottle. Her gaze dropped to the label. "I feel like I'll never get my act together, even though I've been sober for years. Even though I can hold this bottle right now and not want to drink."

They both stared at it. It was amazing that such a tiny object held the power to destroy lives.

"My morning devotion was on Psalm 69," Kathryn said. "In it, the waters came up to the psalmist's neck. He's sinking. There's no foothold. He's weary. He's waiting on God." Her voice cracked. Why could she apply all the right things to Tiff but not know them for herself? "'Answer me,' the psalmist says. Not because he deserves it. Not because he has earned it, but because the steadfast love of the Lord is good."

"I'm familiar with it," Tiff nodded. "I might not be

able to quote the psalm, but I know it ends with an expectation of deliverance."

"Deliverance from this?" Kathryn lifted the bottle between them as the distinct click of a camera sounded in the bushes. She froze. "Who's there?"

A rustle. Then a figure darted out. Kathryn jumped to her feet, but Tiff grabbed her arm. "Let it go."

The figure ran off, disappearing into the neighborhood. Kathryn glared at Tiff. "I could have caught him!"

"To what end? We don't know who that was or what they were doing here, but we both know how easy it is for things to turn ugly if we give into our anger or our pain."

Kathryn closed her eyes. An image of tomorrow's potential headlines flashed before her. *Two misfits drown their sorrows in Sycamore Park.* That would convince her friends she was fine.

Kathryn gripped the skinny neck of the bottle. Every muscle in her body tensed. Even though it was only a few seconds, it felt like an eternity before she made up her mind. "We don't need this." She unscrewed the cap and emptied it on the ground.

Tiff nodded approvingly, but she bit her bottom lip as the bottle drained.

Kathryn slid the now empty container back into the damp paper sleeve. "Everything will be all right. No matter what happens, everything will be fine because there's light at the end of every tunnel."

"What if that light's a train?"

"What if it's hope?"

Tiff's gaze dropped.

"Maybe it doesn't matter if it's a train as long as you're not standing on the tracks when it comes through."

Tiff stuffed her hands into her pockets. "I don't know what I would have done today. Thanks for stopping. For caring."

Kathryn got it. It didn't matter how many years had passed, and it didn't matter that the cravings themselves had weakened. Her body remembered the warm burn of alcohol and its promise to help her forget.

"You need a distraction. Why don't you film for me today?"

"I thought Gloria was filming?"

"She was, but she and Owen have hospital visitations in Grander." Besides, Kathryn wanted a bit more space from her friends. She needed to figure out her next move now that the book deal was gone. And since she would most certainly lose the fan competition, she had to decide if salvaging her career was something she even wanted.

"Thanks."

Kathryn nodded. "Anytime." Because it was about more than her. She finally saw that.

Chapter Ten

E li than strode down the sidewalk. Streetlamps illuminated the early dusk. He'd spent the day chewing on everything that had happened. After Jackson filed the report of the break in, Ethan sent Meg home, because he decided to keep the shop closed until he could be sure his unwanted visitor hadn't sabotaged anything else on his visit.

Ethan checked in with his parents. His dad was recovering from his fall, and surprisingly had little to say about Ethan's predicament. The retirement scam had served his dad a huge helping of humble pie, and Dad kept his business advice to himself.

Still, Ethan knew if this roasting thing was ever going to cut the mustard, he had to expose his tormentor. So much had occurred in the last few days that his mind spun, and since he processed best in the kitchen, that's where he was headed. He'd given Kathryn the space she'd asked for and kept his distance all day. But how long was enough? He itched to seek her out, to let her know that he loved her no matter what, but the velvet box that would prove his love was still tucked inside the cupboard at the bakery.

Mom had asked him why he hadn't given Kathryn the ring, and she didn't agree that he needed to make the proposal *an experience*. She kept saying he should just propose, but he couldn't. It had to be perfect. Kathryn lived online, and this had to be social media worthy. Besides, Kathryn was the one life choice his dad approved of.

No, that wasn't quite right. Dad had said he was proud of how Ethan researched the coffee business before investing. If their relationship was ever going to improve, Ethan needed to start taking his dad at his word and believe him.

Thunder rolled. The stormy day had spilled into the evening, and it suited his mood. Dark, black, and angry. Angry at the people harassing Kathryn online. Angry at the people messing with his bakery. Angry at, well, everything. Nothing had gone according to plan. He couldn't stop what was happening to Kathryn. He couldn't fix his relationship with his dad. He couldn't repair the broken software or stop whoever had targeted his shop. But he could keep things simple and do one thing right. What could be simpler or more right than the Muffin Man proposing by hiding the ring inside a muffin?

Ethan unlocked the bakery door and went directly to

the cupboard. He removed the ring and slipped it into his front pocket. Another stormy rumble vibrated in his chest. If Ethan didn't know for certain that Addison and Eli had also worked from home today, he'd have thought they were dragging their office furniture around upstairs.

Ethan patted his pocket as he strode to the kitchen to set the oven to preheat. As he collected ingredients, a sense of unease settled over him. Something was wrong. The early aroma of freshly roasting beans wafted in the air. His gaze zipped to the lit green light on the coffee roaster. Why was it on? He wasn't roasting anything. He fumbled the muffin cups and dropped them. As he bent over to retrieve them, a deafening roar exploded. The sharp sting of a blast radiated through his body. It knocked Ethan off balance and threw him down. Pain and shock hit like a wall. His ears rang. His chest ached, and a thick fog clouded his vision. Everything moved in a hazy, slow motion.

An eerie silence descended, contrasted only by the roar in his head.

Ethan didn't know how long he lay there. There was no pain. The counter he'd been crouched behind some-what protected him. A penetrating chill numbed him when he should feel heat. He was unable to move—unable to think—until the throbbing of his heart shifted from his chest to his ears. And then another sound—the shrill squealing of an alarm. He rolled to his side and gagged. A sickening scent swirled. The wind tugged his hair.

Wind inside the bakery?

A face appeared. Sudden light. The warmth of hands felt good as they prodded his body. "Ethan!" someone repeated.

It seemed far away, but the feet were right in front of him. *Why was he eye level with feet?*

Jackson's face came into focus. His lips moved.

Jackson had said something, but with his ears ringing, Ethan couldn't understand. He blinked. He pushed himself up.

Jackson grasped him under his arms and helped him. "We gotta get you out of here."

Ethan pieced it together from, "We gotta . . . out . . . here . . ."

Finally upright, Ethan staggered. The roaster had literally exploded. Tables were overturned and hunks of machinery had wedged into the counter he'd been behind. He could have died. Or Meg. Or Eli and Addison. If he'd been open—

He swayed and pressed the butt of his palm to his forehead. *Lord, thank you for protecting us.*

"Is anyone else in here?" Jackson yelled.

Ethan shook his head.

Jackson guided him through the door that wasn't. The blast had blown the glass into pieces. Ethan hobbled across the street. People had started to gather. Emma waited under the covered patio of the restaurant across the street, her black medical bag clutched in her hands.

Someone had pulled the tables apart to make space for an examination. "Sit him here."

Ethan couldn't do anything but obey.

"Can you hear me?"

He shook his head. That hurt. He winced. That also hurt. "Not well."

Jackson hovered as Emma's hands moved over Ethan's limbs, periodically asking with exaggerated enunciation if her touch was painful. Between reading her lips, and the few words that waded through the hum in his ears, Ethan was able to follow the conversation. "You don't appear to have any broken bones, and everything else seems in working order, although you're going to have some impressive bruising tomorrow."

Jackson sagged at Emma's assessment and his eyes briefly closed. "I'm gonna see what I can learn. You're lucky I was here. Someone had called to report a potential break-in at the bakery, and I had just pulled up when the place exploded."

Ethan only caught the odd word. *Lucky* was one of them. He nodded, although it wasn't a word he'd have chosen.

The Lord gives and the Lord takes away. There was nothing in there about luck.

It could have been much worse. They could have been open and serving customers.

Ethan tried to stand, but Emma held him down. "Not until I'm finished." She flicked a pen light into his eyes before slipping it into her chest pocket. Then she held out her hands. "Can you squeeze them?"

He wasn't sure what she was assessing, but she seemed pleased, so he must have passed the test.

She crouched at his feet and slipped her hands under his shoes. "Can you press down like you're pushing on two pedals?"

He did.

"Now walk to the edge of the patio and back." She motioned the desired pathway with her hands.

He felt her stare drilling into him with every step.

Seemingly satisfied, she helped him sit back down. After popping the earpieces to her stethoscope into her ears, she pressed the disc against his chest. She listened intently. How she heard anything over the growing crowd and the sirens was beyond him. She looped the scope around her neck and smiled. Her first smile.

Relief rocketed through him. He was going to be okay. "How did you get here so fast?"

"Ben listens to the police scanner. He heard the report about the break-in. We were coming to check it out."

We. Ethan looked around. Ben was snapping pictures.

A spectacular flash lit the sky, and a thunderclap made Emma jump. The crowd pushed closer despite the sudden downpour unleashed by heaven. Constable Stuart James had arrived and beat the growing crowd of spectators back with a scowl that should have terrified them. It softened only when he looked at Ethan.

"Can I follow Jackson?" Ethan asked Emma.

She nodded her consent. "But we're going to the hospital as soon as the ambulance arrives."

Ethan followed Jackson's path. The exterior walls still stood, but much of the glass was gone. The dining room damage looked mostly cosmetic. Tables and chairs were overturned, but nothing was charred. The sprinklers never even came on. The mess radiated from where the coffee roaster had stood. As if on autopilot, he catalogued the damage. Twisted metal was strewn haphazardly in the room. An acrid smell lingered. The kitchen was okay. The counter he'd been crouched behind had moved at least a few inches. Canisters of flour, chocolate chips, and sugar rolled on the floor. He rubbed his chest.

Jackson frowned, and it made his chest hurt more. "Could have been gunpowder in the roaster."

"Gunpowder?" He had to have misheard him. He tugged his earlobe.

"If I'm right," Jackson said, "when the roaster was turned on, the heat caused the gas to expand, causing the explosion."

"Ethan? Ethan?" Kathryn's panicked cry cut through the static in his ears. Kathryn threw her arms around his neck. "Emma called me." She raked her gaze over him. "She said you're okay."

"I am." He burrowed his face into her hair.

"But your bakery—"

He crushed her to his chest. "I know."

Chapter Eleven

K athryn wiped her face on Ethan's shoulder and thanked the Lord for the millionth time that he was okay. When she had rounded the corner and first seen the bakery's damage, her legs buckled. Tiff had practically carried her to Emma, who pointed out Ethan and Jackson inside the bakery.

"I can't do this," Kathryn had said to Emma. Her heart raced. She was having a heart attack. That had to be it.

Emma did a quick assessment, then squeezed Kathryn's upper arms and looked into her eyes, nodding affirmatively as she spoke. "You can. Just take the next step. Do the next thing."

Kathryn mirrored her friend's nodding and then looked at Ethan picking through the wreckage. He was the next thing. Being there for him. Making sure he was okay.

And he was, but the bakery wasn't as lucky.

Kathryn gently touched Ethan's cheek. "Should I call your parents? Someone should watch you through the night and ensure you're really okay."

"He's going to the hospital when the ambulance gets here." Emma had followed Kathryn across the street. She watched them so closely Kathryn briefly wondered if she was withholding a medical concern, but immediately discarded the notion. That would be unethical, and however difficult, Emma always made the ethical choice.

"Good. That's good he's going to the hospital." Kathryn echoed. "I'll call your parents from there. There's no need from them to come to Sycamore Hill to only turn around and go back to Grander's hospital."

"Kathryn? Ethan?" Gloria shouted from the perimeter Stuart had set up. Owen stood behind her with a hand on her shoulder. It was impossible to miss how Gloria frowned at Tiff, who had stayed on the scene but stood off to the side in the rain.

The winch in Kathryn's stomach cranked. Even here, in the wreckage of Ethan's life, Gloria struggled with Tiff's presence. The air practically crackled.

Kim joined Gloria at the barricade, also grimacing in Tiff's direction. Her friends didn't even try to hide their feelings. They probably thought they were being supportive, even protective of Kathryn, but it roused an unexplainable disappointment in her.

"I need you"—Jackson jutted his chin toward Emma —"and you"—he turned to Jackson and included

Kathryn in his stare—"to leave. This isn't a tourist attraction. It's a crime scene."

"Crime?" Kathryn repeated. "It wasn't an accident?" The winch cinched tighter.

"Out." Jackson pointed.

"I came as soon as I heard," Kim said as they approached.

"We were just getting back from Grander. What happened? We heard something like an explosion," Owen said.

Ethan ruffled his already mussed hair. "I'm not sure. I was going to bake muffins when I noticed the roaster was on. That's the last thing I remember."

"You didn't turn it on?"

Ethan shook his head.

The rain failed to deter onlookers, and the sidewalk and people holding umbrellas of all shapes and sizes soon sprinkled the area like imperfect candy sprinkles on a sugar cookie.

Officer Stuart lifted the crime scene tape and allowed their group to stay on the bakery-side of the boundary. The flimsy barricade was the only thing preventing the crowd from descending on Ethan.

Tiff was on the other side.

Their gazes met. Kathryn nodded in response to her unspoken question. Tiff's chin lifted, and she stepped back, letting the outraged crowd swallow her. Kathryn caught bits and pieces.

"I heard it was premeditated."

"Who would do this?"

"It sounded like gunshots."

"It has to be someone we know."

Ben wove through the throng, gathering quotes for the newspaper, reminding Kathryn that she should have been recording. It was her job. But the idea of capitalizing on Ethan's devastation made her stomach heave, followed by a nauseating thought that was almost as distressing as the destruction. *Was that how her friends felt when she recorded them for the news?*

Kathryn had covered the drug scandal that smeared Gloria's name. She filmed Meg holding the protest sign in front of a heritage tree with Eli chanting beside her. When the town divided over the sledding hill, Kathryn was there with her camera, even catching on film the horrid moment when Emma broke her collarbone. And most recently, she'd covered the story of Oliver's kidnapping and return. Her stomach pitched, and she hugged her waist.

As if he sensed her distress, Ethan pulled her into his arms again. She turned into him and couldn't stop the tears, not when he pressed his lips to her temple. Not even when he whispered that it was going to be okay. She was supposed to be consoling him, but everything had flipped.

Emma leaned in to whisper, "This is the next thing. Grief. It's okay."

Kathryn mourned Ethan's loss and her own insensitivity, and sobbed in relief that every one of her friends were standing here beside her, safe and unharmed.

Jackson exited the bakery and tacked crime scene tape over the door's frame before addressing the growing crowd. "If anyone saw anything, or knows anything, please come and speak to me before leaving."

Clara Brisbane flapped her arms from the front of the pack. "There was a man," she said, in partial hysterics. "I called about the break-in."

Jackson lifted the perimeter tape so Clara could come closer.

"He was wearing dark jeans. I saw him through the bakery's window and then on the street right after the explosion." Clara wrung her hands in front of her thick middle. "Are you all okay?" Her worried gaze dragged over each one of them, lingering on Meg.

Of course, Clara was concerned about Meg and the baby. They'd forged a deep, almost familial bond over the last year.

"We're okay. I wasn't here when it happened." Meg rested her hand over her midsection.

Clara's fidgeting relaxed.

"Did this man say anything?" Jackson drew Clara's focus back.

Mrs. Brisbane shook her head. "No, but he was watching the bakery. He came out from the alley as Ethan went in from the front. It was like he knew it was going to happen any second. When Ethan turned on the lights, he started to cross the street like he was going to knock on the door, but then the windows blew out." Her gaze bounced between Jackson and Ethan. "I've never seen him before."

If Clara didn't recognize the man, that meant he wasn't a local. Clara knew everyone.

"We need to find this guy," Jackson said. "If he's not involved, he may be able to tell us what happened." Jackson pointed her toward Stuart and waved to get the man's attention. "Can you get her full statement?"

Stuart gave a two-fingered salute.

A horn beeped, and the crowd parted to let the ambulance from Grander through. "It's time," Emma said.

"I'll go with you." Kathryn followed Ethan to the ambulance.

Emma shared her assessment on Ethan with the medic opening the bay doors and helped Ethan inside. Her report sent a million and one waves of gratefulness through Kathryn. It could have been so much worse.

Kathryn joined Ethan in the ambulance once they got him sitting on the gurney and Emma had exited. Emma reached back and squeezed Kathryn's hand. "I'm praying."

"Thank you."

Emma left.

"I'm Simon," the medic said. "I'll be with you the whole way to Grander. This is my partner, Cassie. She's driving."

Cassie appeared at the back of the open bay doors and gave a little wave.

Kathryn bit the inside of her cheek. Simon's laid-back tone was a touch too mellow. Shouldn't Cassie be behind the wheel with the sirens screaming, racing them to the hospital? Shouldn't Simon be doing something more? But she didn't voice any of that. Instead, she said, "Hi."

Simon maintained strong eye contact with her, and she realized he was doing something. He was trying to assess whether or not he'd have two patients to treat. After a few more uncomfortable seconds, he shifted his full attention to Ethan. "Can you hold your arms out horizontally, palms up?"

Ethan did.

"Good. Now close your eyes."

It seemed like a preschool game. *Simon says hold out your arms. Simon says close your eyes.*

Simon tapped Ethan's shoulder.

Ethan opened his eyes, and his gaze immediately found hers. "It's not your fault," he said.

Her chin quivered. "Ever since I let my name stand in the contest—"

"Not your fault," he repeated.

"Lay on your back." Simon helped Ethan into a supine position and bent his knees to thirty degrees. He flexed both of Ethan's knees and rested one on the gurney. He extended the other and allowed it to drop. Then he repeated the steps with the other leg. He continued with his evaluation as Cassie handed him instruments and added the occasional comment.

"Is he okay?" Kathryn asked.

"I think so," Cassie answered. "We need to take him to the hospital for further testing. Would you like to ride in the front with me?"

"Okay." She gently pressed her lips to Ethan's. "I'll see you when we get there."

Kathryn buckled into the front passenger seat as Cassie put the ambulance in gear. She didn't turn on the sirens. That had to be a good sign.

The ride to Grander was awkward despite the easy-going attitude of Simon's partner. Cassie had fallen silent when it became clear Kathryn didn't want to chat. All Kathryn wanted was a promise that Ethan would be okay, but she knew the woman couldn't give her that. So, there was nothing to say.

They drove out of the storm. Eventually, even the pinging of raindrops ceased. The clouds kept rolling and an occasional thunderclap rumbled, but it sounded more and more distant each time.

The ambulance rocked as Cassie stopped in front of the hospital's emergency entrance.

Kathryn hopped out. She immediately grabbed hold of Ethan's hand and walked alongside the gurney as they entered the hospital. A doctor joined the team, and Simon updated him.

"I want a CT head and chest X-ray," the doctor said.

Ethan tightened his grip on her hand.

They aimed the gurney toward double doors, and a nurse stopped Kathryn. She lost her hold on Ethan, and before she could react, he was gone.

"It'll take about thirty minutes for the test, and then the doctor will need to review the results. You can wait there." The nurse pointed to the waiting room they'd breezed past. "Or, the cafeteria is open."

Kathryn's chest was too tight to answer. She watched through the window in the door until Ethan disappeared around the corner. Then she made her way to the cafeteria. After buying a coffee, she chose a table in the back. With her elbows on the table, she pressed her forehead into the butt of her palms.

"It'll be okay." Kathryn had to believe Ethan would be fine and his business would recover. They couldn't give up on The Muffin Man. Ethan came alive in his bakery in a way that Kathryn could only hope to imitate one day. She enjoyed her job. She did good work. But she didn't thrive in it like Ethan. When he interacted with customers, created new recipes, or catered custom orders for events, she knew she witnessed the fulfillment of 1 Corinthians 10:31. *Whether you eat or drink or whatever you do, do all to the glory of God.* Ethan baked to the glory of God. His business was his platform for serving others. It was never just about him. He paused and prayed with staff and customers, he generously sponsored a children's soccer team, and he hosted game nights for Sycamore Hill Community Church's youth group. The bakery had to be salvageable. The town needed it.

Just do the next thing. Kathryn sucked in a breath. The next thing was hard.

She called Ethan's parents and looped them in. She didn't know how long she sat there staring at the coffee she never drank, but when her phone dinged, she assumed it was Shannon and Grant. They were probably here and looking for her. When she glanced at the screen, her heart seized.

Distasteful social media comments were creating an explosion bigger than the one that took out The Muffin Man. One person even posted song lyrics in the past tense. *Did you know the muffin man, the muffin man, the muffin man?* She tossed her phone on the table and pulled up her shirt collar to cover her chin and nose. A bitter tang filled her mouth. How were these sorts of comments the fruit of her labor? What was she giving her life to? How did 1 Corinthians 10:31 play out in her world?

"Kathryn?"

Her head snapped up. "Mr. and Mrs. Roberts." She stood. "They took Ethan for some tests. He should be back anytime."

"He's already back. We spoke with the doctor."

Already back? How long had she been sitting here?

"They're releasing him. He has to follow up with an ears, nose, and throat specialist and the family doctor in a week."

She sagged. *Thank you, Lord, for one million and two reasons.*

Shannon wrapped an arm around Kathryn's shoulder and guided her out of the cafeteria. "This has been a long day already. Why don't you come home with us? It's almost dinner time, and you shouldn't be alone, and Ethan's staying with us for a few days so we can watch him."

In less than thirty minutes, they were in Shannon and Grant's living room, drinking hot beverages. Gloria promised to pack an overnight bag for Kathryn and drop it off later. In the meantime, Kathryn had changed into a borrowed pair of jogging pants and a hoodie. Everyone looked exhausted. Shannon and Grant peppered Ethan with questions, but Kathryn couldn't live through the telling another time. "Why don't I make us something to eat?" She stood. "How do omelettes sound?" Kathryn had been in the Roberts' home enough times to feel comfortable making the offer.

"That would be lovely, thank you." Shannon smiled at her.

Kathryn went into the kitchen, pulled out a small cutting board, and started chopping an onion and a few small peppers for omelettes. She opened the fridge and rummaged around, looking for the salsa. She knocked over a corked bottle of wine, and the chaos in her mind screamed to a halt. Desire hit like a wave. It happened like this sometimes. Coming from nowhere and stealing the breath from her lungs. Her fingers tingled at the memory of dumping the cheap wine with the twist-off cap in the park. She felt a sharp pang of regret, the kind she hadn't felt in a very long time.

Kathryn slammed the fridge. Now working quickly, she sliced through the vegetables until they were finely diced. More than finely diced. Minced would be more accurate. Anything to keep her mind off the smooth feel of the glass bottle, the crackle of the paper encasing it, the sweet scent of its contents gushing over the rim as she dumped it.

"It's not going to help." She had to convince her betraying senses. "One drink *can* hurt me. It *will* hurt me."

Her hands trembled. The bottle pulled like clickbait.

Chapter Twelve

An ache tightened the back of Ethan's throat. When he left his parents in the living room to check on Kathryn, he didn't expect to find her like this. Harsh fluorescent lights illuminated her pale skin, and a single bottle of booze sat on the table in front of her. She wasn't touching it. The cork was in place. But she was fixated on it. Tension thickened the air. He didn't know anything about addiction, but he knew in his gut this moment mattered. What he said and did next would impact their relationship forever.

Ethan moved as if he were approaching a frightened animal. He knelt on the floor by her chair. He didn't touch her. He kept his voice gentle and low. "Kathryn?"

Her gaze zipped to his. The cord in her neck throbbed with a pulse. Her hands—that had been clasped in her lap, writhing and twisting—stilled. She looked terrified.

If Ethan had one wish, it would be to melt the fear from her face and the anxiety from her body and replace it with confidence and joy. His single wish would be for her, not his destroyed business. He knew enough about addiction to understand he couldn't fight it for her, but he could stand with her. He would do everything within his power to ensure that she knew she would never again stand alone.

Kathryn's eyes brimmed, but determination shone through as well. She dampened her lips and nodded slowly, as if coming to some kind of understanding in her head. With her chin high, she inhaled hard. "I saw this in the fridge."

He remained quiet.

"I wouldn't be able to sleep here knowing this bottle was here. So, I took it out."

He reached for her hand. She didn't pull away, and he counted that as a win.

"Then I realized it wasn't mine. Not mine to drink. Not mine to dump." She shrugged, snorted, and let out a raw laugh all at once. "Then I didn't know what to do."

He swallowed the lump wedged in his throat. "Thank you for sharing that. I imagine it's not easy."

She pressed her lips together until they became a thin, white line. Pinching her eyes closed, she took another breath before shaking free of his hold. She pushed back from the table and stood. She didn't reach for the bottle, but Ethan could see the struggle.

After a shaky step backward, she strode to the

counter. She leaned her hip against it and folded her arms across her chest. "I've ruined everything." Her voice wobbled. "Maybe you'd be better off without me."

Ethan's heart jolted. He couldn't imagine life without Kathryn. He moved in front of her. The energy humming between them could have powered the house. He looked into her eyes, trying to convey love and strength. "Never," he said softly. "I'd never be better without you. If I had to pick between the shop and you, I choose you. Every time and in every way."

A sad smile curled her lips. "I've spent my whole life believing no one would ever choose me."

His head swayed in disagreement. "Not true. Tiff chose you. Your friends chose you. And most importantly, God chooses you. Every drink. Every poor decision. Every sin. It's been nailed to the cross because He chose you."

Kathryn caught her lower lip between her teeth. Her features softened, and the tears she'd been blinking back rolled down her cheeks.

"He knows you fully." Ethan spoke as he approached slowly. "Every thought, every desire, every action, and every failure. He loves you anyway." Ethan snagged her hand and tugged gently, giving her enough time to pull away if she desired. When she didn't resist him, he wrapped his arms around her. *Lord, help me to love her well.*

She buried her face into his chest. They stood like that, quietly and contentedly, until she whispered into his shirt, "What if I never fully recover? What if every crisis brings it back?"

She didn't have to define *it*. It was the secret she'd carried for far too long. It was the thing she'd allowed to define her. The thing she wanted no one to know but now everyone knew. He tipped his head and spoke into her hair. "Then we face it together."

He wanted to say something more, but words failed him. He wanted to tell her he understood her pain, that he'd take it away if he could. Overwhelmed by a sense of responsibility to protect and guide and love her no matter what, he tightened his arms and let his presence be his offering. Ethan rubbed small circles on her back as she wept, crying so hard he wondered if this was the first time she'd ever let herself grieve.

"Thank you for not leaving," she whispered. "For not believing the worst."

He cupped her chin in his palm and lifted her face. "You don't have to thank me." He tucked a strand of hair around her ear with his other hand. "I love you."

She wiped away the last drop of dampness from her cheeks and straightened up just as someone cleared their throat in the doorway.

His father stood frozen in place. His face lit with worry but also filled with awe. He'd held back Ethan's mother, who seemed about to burst. When Dad let her go, Mom rushed to Kathryn, but Dad held his gaze with a look Ethan couldn't quite identify. "You're a good man, Ethan. I'm proud of you."

Ethan couldn't breathe. He didn't realize how desperately he'd wanted to hear those words from his father until an invisible weight lifted from his chest. *His dad was proud of him.* Not for swinging a hammer or for fixing a car, but for loving Kathryn well. Mom had been right all along.

Mom fussed over Kathryn as Dad quietly and unobtrusively uncorked the wine and dumped it down the sink. Ethan's entire body relaxed. His parents chose Kathryn, too.

"Do you want to talk about it?" His mom led Kathryn back to the table and offered her a seat. Dad put on the kettle and removed hot chocolate and several varieties of tea from the cupboard. It was the most domestic action Ethan had ever seen his dad take.

Kathryn explained everything—the pranks pulled on her during the contest, the bullying online, the cancelation of her book, and Tiff showing up and complicating her life. She said things Ethan didn't even know. It was as if now that the secret was out, it all had to come out.

Once Kathryn finished, she smiled. Really smiled. Her eyes looked lighter and her countenance brighter. "I had no idea how heavy that was to carry alone. I'd gotten used to it."

"We aren't meant to do life alone," Dad said. "We need each other."

Ethan's mouth dropped. Who was this man? His dad never spoke of community or needing others unless it was to fill the roster of a ball team.

"Considering everything that's happened at the bakery," Dad continued, "do you think the police should know about the online harassment? It seems small when we consider it in isolation, but altogether—" Dad shook his head. "I don't believe in coincidences."

"The timing is suspicious," Kathryn agreed, "but the person did nothing illegal."

Ethan's cell phone rang. "It's Jackson." After a quick conversation, they disconnected. "He wants us to come back to the bakery in the morning."

"We can drop you off, or if you prefer, we can drive to Sycamore Hill tonight to pick up one of your vehicles."

"All of us," Ethan clarified. "Jackson wants to see all of us."

Chapter Thirteen

The time it took for Ethan's dad to find a parking spot gave Kathryn a few extra minutes to settle the butterflies in her stomach. They had to park two blocks over from the bakery, which didn't make sense. The road should have been cleared by now.

"Look at the people." Shannon's mouth gaped. "This can't be because of the bakery. Not still."

"I think it is." Kathryn pointed to the crime tape that still barricaded a section of sidewalk. The street was clear, however, traffic slowed as gawkers crept by.

As they hurried down the sidewalk, the persistent scent of dust clung to the back of Kathryn's throat. It was faint, like the lingering aroma of a campfire. Even the air felt too warm for a late spring day, despite a weak breeze coming from the direction of the pond.

Kathryn snuck a glance at Ethan. He remained quiet. But the closer they got to the bakery, the tighter he squeezed her hand. It felt good to be needed. To be the person giving something rather than being the one always taking it.

Any doubts about Ethan's commitment to her had vanished yesterday, wiped away by his gentleness and love. But alongside that certainty came conviction. Kathryn should never have doubted him or her friends. She'd allowed the enemy a foothold in her mind, and he'd thrown a party. Her cheeks burned just thinking of how she sat in front of the bottle debating, wondering, desiring, and hating herself. The enemy condemned God's children, but Kathryn was learning there was a massive difference between conviction and condemnation. If she'd learned anything in her battle for sobriety, it was that the Lord convicted his children to prompt repentance and change. His lovingkindness led to a repentance that removed guilt, not heaped it on.

Jackson, Stuart, Ben, and Tiff waited outside the bakery on the sidewalk. As soon as he saw them approaching, Stuart met them at the boundary and pulled the crime scene tape aside to let them into the inner sanctum. Someone had knocked out the remaining shards of glass that clung to the window frame, leaving just the rectangular opening. Someone had also cleared the glass that had spilled onto the street. Several people moved about inside. Tiff held a camera.

Ben pointed at it. "She might have video of the guy Clara Brisbane mentioned."

"I called Clara over as well." Jackson looked at his watch. "She'll be here any minute."

"You were filming?" Kathryn blinked several times. She hadn't asked Tiff to record anything.

"I hope you don't mind that I recorded for you. I wasn't sure what you might need for your show."

"It gets better." Ben leaned forward, eagerness spilling out. "Tell them the rest."

At Ben's encouraging nod, Tiff grew more animated and confident. "After we met in Grander at the coffee shop, I secretly set up a nighttime camera to catch you coming and going from the bakery."

Kathryn gasped. "You never told me that."

Tiff's cheeks reddened. "I was only going to tell you if I caught something worthwhile for your show." She lifted her shoulders sweetly. "I didn't know I couldn't record audio."

"Either way, her ignorance might have broken the case," Jackson said.

Tiff cast a quick look in Jackson's direction. "I didn't realize the potential legal implications until Jackson told me." She shrugged. "Reality TV shows do it all the time."

"With consent," Stuart said.

Tiff tugged her lips between her teeth. Jackson took the camera from her and began scrolling through the feed.

"Officer McGregor!" Clara waved her hand from outside the crime scene tape.

"I'll get her." Stuart let Clara in and escorted her to their group.

"Is this who you saw?" Jackson turned the screen to Clara.

"Yes!" Clara's sausage log of a forehead curl bounced with her head bobbing.

"Do you recognize him?" Jackson turned the screen so Kathryn and Ethan could see it.

The hope that had been building in Kathryn's chest plummeted. "No, I don't."

"I might." Ethan squinted. "Can you zoom in on his collar?"

Jackson rotated the camera to Tiff, who zoomed in for him.

Ethan jabbed his finger at the screen. "He's wearing the same pin on his collar."

"Who?" Kathryn asked.

"He came to The Muffin Man the day we found those stones mixed in with the coffee beans. He said he was there to buy a coffee."

Kathryn's jaw loosened. "I remember him. He tried to push in when you said you were closed."

Ethan took a step away and spun on his heel. After a few seconds, he faced them again. "Why would he target me?"

"Maybe he showed up to watch the fallout of his handiwork, and when you closed the shop to livestream for my channel, you robbed him of that?"

"Do you know who he is?" Shannon asked.

Shannon and Grant had been so quiet that Kathryn had forgotten they were there.

"No, but his information is on the shop's computer. I appeased the guy with a punch card for free coffee, so when he came in to claim the first one, he had to register. He's been back several times."

"Where's the computer now?" Grant looked dubiously at the shop.

"Addison and Eli took it home to try and fix the program."

Kathryn's gaze collided with Ethan's and held. His whole demeanor changed as understanding and then relief flooded his frame. "They took it home. They'll be able to recover the information. We got him."

"It's unlikely he registered with the real name." Jackson frowned.

"Why would he do this?" Ethan blew out a frustrated sound and Kathryn threaded her fingers with his. A small part of her still feared the bakery misfortune was connected to the contest.

Ben's gaze drilled into her. "I interviewed this guy. He runs the wholesale coffee bean business, Cool Beans. I should have noticed something was off."

Ethan jerked at the company's name. "I went there. I had considered ordering my beans from him before I decided to invest in a roaster."

"Tell me more about this place." Jackson jotted down the company name.

"I didn't meet this guy. I spoke with a woman. Cool

Beans is a little more than halfway between Grander and here. It's a small business. They roast beans in the garage and ship their product locally."

"And I was promoting your marketing plan to ship coffee bean orders directly to customers," Kathryn finished. It was all starting to make sense.

"I got the feeling he'd been watching Ethan for a while," Ben said. "Worried some of his marketing strategies were going to overshadow him."

"But I wasn't a threat to him. I wasn't moving into the wholesale market. I was targeting customers, not businesses."

"There is no way he could have known that," said Kathryn.

Ben's mouth tightened. "I should have seen this coming."

"It's not your fault," Ethan told him.

"That's what I keep saying." Emma looped her arm through Ben's. Gloria, Owen, and Kim had exited the bakery behind her. It was almost comical, the way they filed through the doorway despite the huge opening where the window used to be.

"That's enough for me to track him down and bring him in for questioning."

Tiff's mouth tightened as they neared. But, instead of pushing Tiff out, the group widened the circle and let her in.

Kathryn welled up. There was something different about her friends. Something that felt helpful and not judgmental. But she couldn't put her finger on what had changed. They were acting like they always did. Maybe the person who changed was her? Maybe what she previously saw as judgemental and harsh was her looking at her friends through the wrong lens?

"What is everyone doing here?" Ethan's eyebrows shot up. He looked at Jackson. "I thought the crime scene tape meant you were still investigating."

"No, we're done, but your dad asked us to leave it up for a bit. At least until the new window goes in."

"My dad?" Ethan echoed.

"I'm probably needed inside." Grant's mysterious smile revealed nothing as he turned to slip into the store, but Shannon's shiny cheeks and twinkling eyes looked more mischievous than a toddler sneaking a cookie.

"Hold up." Jackson stopped them. "I have something for you as well."

Grant stuffed his hands into his front pockets and rolled onto his toes and then back onto his heels. Kathryn noted how he avoided looking at Ethan. Something was afoot.

"Thanks to the picture Kathryn took that morning at the diner in Grander, we caught the guy who scammed you."

Shannon gasped and grabbed onto Grant's arm.

Jackson grinned. "I contacted the fraud unit, and they had a lead on the guy. They caught up with him. The judge will likely suspend the sentence if he repays everybody, and guys like this usually do to avoid jail.

Thankfully, he hasn't spent the funds yet, so you'll likely get it all back."

Mom threw her hands into the air. "Hallelujah! Thank you, Jackson!"

Jackson grinned. "Don't thank me, thank Kathryn. Without her photograph, we wouldn't have found him. The name he gave you was bogus, and his business front has been deserted."

Shannon threw her arms around Kathryn, laughing and crying.

Kathryn met Jackson's eyes over Shannon's shoulder. He smiled as he said, "I thought you all might be ready for some good news."

Thank you, she mouthed.

"Thank you." Grant vigorously shook Jackson's hand, clasping his arm, then repeated the action with Stuart. He wiped his eyes. Kathryn thought he even stood a little taller.

"Not to put a damper on the celebration," Gloria interrupted, twisting her lips into a frown. "But has anyone been online?" She wiggled her cell.

Kathryn's stomach twisted. They were announcing the winner of the Fan Favorite Choice Award today. She'd hoped her friends would forget. "It wasn't me, was it?"

"What wasn't you?" Shannon pulled a tissue from her purse and wiped her eyes.

Gloria shook her head. "I'm sorry. You didn't win." Ethan touched her arm. "I'm sorry, too."

Kathryn waited for disappointment to fall. And waited some more. She must be numb. "How bad is it?"

"Someone posted a picture of you holding a bottle in the park with Tiffany. The comments are awful."

Tiff gulped. "I'm sorry, Kathryn. That's my fault."

Kathryn's heart dipped, not over losing the contest, but over the idea that Tiff might add this to the burden she carried. She squared her shoulders. "So what if I lost the contest? So what if perfect strangers draw the wrong conclusions about what was a huge victory for us. We have what really matters." Kathryn looped her arms through Gloria and Kim's. "Friends that care, and friends that we care about." She held Tiff's watery gaze. "That includes you."

Tiff gave the tiniest nod.

"Why don't you tell them, Tiff?" Gloria nodded at Tiff.

Kathryn caught her breath. Gloria had called her *Tiff*. Not *that girl*.

Tiff's smile faltered, but only for a second. "You guys need to come inside."

Ethan's arm circled her waist. "Why? What are you all doing here, and why did Dad ask to leave the crime scene tape up?"

"We have a surprise." Emma's gesture indicated that Kathryn and Ethan should follow them.

The interior had been swept clean. Tables and chairs were stacked neatly in the back. But the immediate area surrounding the roaster still showed scars. Holes of various sizes perforated the counter separating it from the kitchen. Bits of cupcakes and pies even splattered the ceiling. Flour and cookie crumbs dusted every surface like drywall dust. Ethan wrapped a hand around the back of his neck.

"How did you walk away from this?" Shannon's eyes were huge. She hadn't seen the scene until now, and the reality that Ethan could have been killed nearly buckled her.

"I was behind the counter."

The destroyed counter. Kathryn's stomach heaved. Grant cleared his throat, and the horror on Shannon's face was quickly replaced with suppressed excitement. Something was up. Shannon nodded encouragingly at Grant.

"You know that your mom and I had been looking for passive income to help in our retirement years." Grant addressed Ethan. "We had decided that if Jackson was able to recover any of our money, we wanted to invest it in your coffee business."

Ethan's mouth gaped, and Kathryn slipped her arm through his.

Grant introduced his foreman, Joel. Both of them had huge smiles splitting their faces, and a small crew of men fell in behind them. "Nobody deserves to have their life's work taken from them like this." Grant gestured to the now mostly emptied space. "We're going to rebuild The Muffin Man even better than before."

Ethan screwed up his eyes. Considering all the ways

his father had tried to lure Ethan away from a career as a baker, Kathryn got it. Logic dictated Grant should be dancing on The Muffin Man's grave, but instead, he grieved with his son.

"But you didn't know about the money until just now." Carving a hand through his hair, Ethan held it back and then released it. He eyeballed his dad.

"Once we decided to invest, we also decided it didn't matter if we got the money back or not. We were all in. You are our safest bet. We believe in you, and if you believe in The Muffin Man, then so do we."

Ethan's mouth slackened. When he didn't move, Kathryn nudged him. "Go hug your father."

Ethan stumbled forward, and his dad met him half-way. The two men embraced. "You turned out great in spite of me." Grant's muffled words warmed Kathryn's heart.

They pulled apart, and Grant swiped a backhand across his eyes. "Joel assembled the crew last night, and with Jackson's permission to be on the scene, they've been working non-stop."

"How'd you find a crew?"

"Pastor Owen called some young men at the church, and it turns out there are a few guys looking to apprentice. Once Joel fills out the government forms, we'll have enough workers." His cheeks flushed.

"What about retirement?"

Grant snorted. "There wouldn't be a retirement

without you and Kathryn. I'm sorry it took something like this to bring me around."

"And I'm here to make sure he stays off the ladders." Joel winked.

Mom threaded her arm through Grant's. "We're starting the paperwork so Joel can eventually take over the business and the apprentices. But all this is only if you want it. You don't have to partner with us. What do you want to do, Ethan?"

Kathryn held her breath, and Ethan held his dad's gaze.

"I'm done telling you what you should do," Grant said.

Ethan was positively gobsmacked, and it made Kathryn feel lighter and happier than she ever thought possible. Tears prickled, and Kathryn squeezed Ethan's arm. "What do you think?"

Ethan surveyed the space. His grin started small but soon mirrored his father's. He thrust a fist into the air. "We rebuild!"

Everyone cheered.

CHAPTER 14

One Week Later

"C an you believe my dad?" Ethan pointed across what used to be the bakery's dining area to where his dad ordered around his construction crew. Light-headedness scrambled his brain. He still couldn't believe all that had unfolded.

"It's kind of mind-blowing," Kathryn agreed.

Dad wasn't the only one blowing Ethan's mind. Kathryn hadn't been online since the night they'd announced she'd lost the contest. She hadn't responded to a single comment or question. In fact, she'd deleted the apps from her phone. She blamed the remodel, but they both knew a full schedule had never stopped her before. She had chosen to pull back to gain perspective, and he hadn't seen her happier or healthier despite the disturbing details trickling in as Jackson and Stuart continued to fit the puzzle pieces together.

Shawn—the guy who'd targeted Ethan—had been

watching him for a while, waiting for the opportunity to swap out a premixed bag of beans and pebbles with the ones left by his delivery man near the alley door. Even worse, while Shawn was in claiming his free coffees, he lifted a key from Addison, had a new key cut, then returned Addison's key to be "found" in the bakery. Shawn had the freedom to enter and exit at will, swapping salt for sugar to bomb the cooking show, damage the computer, and add gunpowder to the roaster. The unbelievable details could have filled a crime show episode, yet Kathryn didn't report on a single one.

She'd stayed by his side, swinging a hammer, hanging drywall, and laughing full belly laughs like when they were kids. It was odd; in a crazy way, despite all the losses, this had been the best week of Ethan's life.

Dad's crew had gutted the space in a single day, and the trades had already been in to update the wiring and plumbing. And now, Dad stood over a folding table and studied plans—plans Ethan had drawn up years ago when he'd been dreaming about what he'd do to the bakery if he ever had the time and money to renovate.

Just a few months ago, Ethan would have never thought this moment was possible. Back then, his dad was more likely to tease him about his work than encourage him. Now, here they were, in the ruins of The Muffin Man, making his dreams come true. The difficulty of the last few weeks had really been an opportunity in disguise—an opportunity to work with his dad and craft something that reflected the best of both of them. This was something they would both be proud of.

"The only shock bigger than seeing your dad here is seeing them together." Kathryn pointed her chin in Tiff and Gloria's direction.

All his friends had been showing up daily to do whatever labor they could. Gloria, in her collared shirt and khaki pants, and Tiff in a pair of dark jeans and a graphic t-shirt, chatted as they measured and cut drywall. The women couldn't be more different. When Gloria placed her hand over Tiff's and they bowed their heads as if to pray, Kathryn tightened her hold on Ethan's hand.

Ethan planted a kiss on her temple. "It's not fair," he said softly. "Everyone is getting what they wanted but you."

Kathryn lifted onto her tiptoes and lightly brushed her lips against his. "That's not true."

Before she could elaborate, a police cruiser parked out front, and Jackson approached with a somber expression. "Can I grab you two for a minute?"

They followed Jackson outside.

"We have some news about the threats and bullying Kathryn received online."

Kathryn stiffened. "I didn't know you were still looking into that."

"I know you were very concerned that your participation in the contest was somehow to blame for Ethan's misfortune. I can tell you with one hundred percent assurance that concern is unfounded."

Any rigidity left in Kathryn's posture evaporated, and Ethan relaxed. Fully relaxed. She was going to be okay.

"I never believed it was connected," Ethan said.

"I wouldn't say they were disconnected," Jackson corrected him. "The events are connected, just not in the way that you thought."

A chill swept over Ethan. He bit the inside of his cheek.

"I poked around on several social media platforms, and I found your bully." Jackson looked Kathryn in the eyes. "She and Ethan's saboteur are in a relationship." Jackson showed Kathryn and Ethan a picture of the girl.

Ethan shuffled back a step. "That's the woman I spoke with at Cool Beans." The implications of this discovery hit like an anvil. *It was his fault.* "My misfortune wasn't connected to your contest." He looked at Kathryn. "Your misfortune was connected to me."

Jackson nodded. "They cooked up this idea when you announced your plans to start a coffee bean subscription service. They thought if they could discredit Kathryn while she was trying to promote you, they'd also discredit you, and no one would make the connection back to them."

"I can't believe it." Ethan felt dizzy. "I'm so sorry."

"I don't know if this helps," Jackson said, "but they didn't know you'd be in the bakery when the roaster exploded. When Shawn saw the announcement that you were closing for the day due to the break in, he used his key to let himself back in. He even waited until the adjacent businesses closed. They didn't plan to hurt anyone."

"Was he there when Ethan arrived?"

Jackson nodded.

So he *had* heard someone moving around! Ethan had assumed it was thunder.

"Shawn put in the gunpowder, turned on the roaster, and hurried out the back door."

"And he had no idea I'd come in the front door," Ethan murmured.

"That's why he was there in the aftermath. He blended in with the crowd because he needed to see that you were okay."

"And that's why Clara saw him." Kathryn finished with a snort. "How could anyone be dumb enough to think heating gunpowder wouldn't hurt anyone?"

"Gunpowder burns very quickly because the potassium nitrate supplies oxygen to the charcoal and sulfur, accelerating the burn rate. This combustion creates a gas more dangerous than the actual gunpowder. Had they heated it in the open air, the gas would have just expanded into the air," Jackson explained.

"But since it was trapped in the roaster—" Ethan started.

"It forced its way out with an explosion much bigger than they anticipated," Jackson finished.

They all looked at the bakery in silence.

Jackson shifted gears. "I got in touch with the awards coordinator, and after updating them on virtual stalking and harassment laws, they announced a plan to reorganize before next year's contest. But it doesn't change anything for you this year, Kathryn."

"That's okay." Kathryn said it in a way that Ethan really believed her. It really was okay.

"Let me know if you need anything else," Jackson said, before leaving.

"Are you really okay with this?" Ethan needed to hear it again.

Kathryn hugged her middle and surveyed the storefront. "I am. You know, great things have come from this. Things that might not have been had the details unfolded any other way. How can I be anything but thankful? God took what the enemy meant for evil and turned it around and used it for good."

On the other side of Ethan's newly installed window, Gloria and Tiff chatted. Gloria threw her head back and laughed as Tiff gestured animatedly. His dad stuffed a drill in the appropriate holster on his tool belt, as Eli and Addison, with Ethan's computer tucked under his arm, descended the stairs. It was working out for everybody but Kathryn. Ethan wanted good for her as well. "You amaze me."

She turned into his arms and leaned her cheek against his chest. Maybe his problem was he was trying to define what good meant. Maybe he needed to let God define it? He breathed in the familiar scent of her shampoo. The sun glinted off the gilded Muffin Man sign that someone had scrubbed clean and rehung. As their friends worked inside, the occasional shout of laughter trickled out. For one blazing moment, everything was perfect.

Ethan motioned for Kathryn to go into the bakery ahead of him. They walked through the newly installed door that was even nicer than the previous one. As they approached his father, Ethan slapped a hand on his back. "Let me see these kitchen plans."

Dad tucked a pencil behind his ear. "I was thinking, why not expand a bit more?" He pointed at the space between the wall of ovens and the sink. "If we pushed this wall back and widened this gap, you could add a nice-sized prep counter in the middle."

Ethan's throat squeezed. His dad was not only helping him rebuild, but was designing the space with Ethan's needs in mind. It really was a miracle. "I'm not sure I can afford it. The insurance came through, but I'm pinching pennies already."

"When we get our money back, your mother and I are putting it into the bakery."

Ethan's father unfolded an updated design. It had all the details of Ethan's original dream, but expanded. Ethan's lungs compressed.

"If we move the cafe area near the back"—Dad pointed to the drawings—"we can include a wall of built-ins that hold board games and a mini library or book-store. Customers can grab coffee or lunch and linger."

Kathryn's eyes sparkled. "And what about evening events? That's typically the slowest time of day, but if you did that, you'd have space to host things like art classes, poetry reading, open mic nights. You'd be the hub of activity for local artists. You could even host recovery meetings here after hours instead of in the church basement."

"All subject to your approval, of course," Dad said.

"I think it sounds wonderful," Ethan said. "More than wonderful. It's amazing."

Kathryn beamed her first high-wattage smile that wasn't aimed at a camera. The Muffin Man wasn't just becoming his dream business, it was becoming theirs. His dad smiled proudly, as if he'd known from day one things were going to be this way—him redesigning the bakery, Kathryn providing insights, Ethan living his best life. The bells above the door jingled, and everyone lifted their faces.

Meg's cheeks flushed as she balanced on the top of a small stepladder. "It didn't feel right to not hear the bells."

Ethan thought he might burst. This was his family. It was more than those related by blood but included those connected together through friendship—he gazed at Kathryn—and love.

CHAPTER 15
Two Months Later

Tiff gave Kathryn a thumbs up, and Kathryn looked at the camera, dead centre. "It's been a few months since I've been online, and it's finally time I addressed the crazy comments. No, I did not check into rehab. No, my relationship with Ethan didn't end. I pulled back to give the trolls time to move on. I pulled back to gain some much-needed distance so I could gain some much-needed perspective. I was in front of the camera so often that I had forgotten who I really was, and it had impacted my mental health negatively. You've never seen me like this before, makeup free, no filter, just plain Kathryn. I decided my last episode had to be this way for a specific reason."

Ethan approached from behind Tiff, and Kathryn looked past the camera to catch his eye. His beaming smile of approval gave her all the courage she needed.

"Many of us, me included, present an online personality that is disconnected from reality. We only show the perfect us. The filtered us. The us we wish we could be. But no one is perfect. In my attempt to livestream during the Fan Favourite Choice Awards, you saw my flaws. You saw parts of me that I didn't want anybody to see. But God used that exposure to do a work in my heart. He used it to rebuild me."

Kathryn lifted her phone so it was in the frame and paused to read the screen. "Yes, the contest impacted Ethan's bakery. Yes, he has to rebuild from scratch."

She flicked her gaze back to the camera. "I'm reading your comments as my friend films so we can dialogue. I appreciate your concern for Ethan's bakery and for what happened to me, but the hate toward the culprit is not necessary. It needs to stop. *Name and shame* is not a trend I want on my feed, so all posts with that feel have been and will be deleted."

She read a few more comments. A smile softened her face. "No, I won't DM anyone the details so you can take care of it for me."

More comments popped up on the phone newsfeed.

We love you, Kathryn.

I knew you could never relapse.

I missed your channel.

And then finally, one she had been hoping for.

Praying for. The reason she was making the change to speak more openly about addiction, mental health, and the daily struggle to live clean. Someone named Still-Falling wrote:

I've followed your channel for years, and as I saw your story unfold, I felt hope for the first time. If you can get your life back together after addiction, maybe I can too.

Pressure grew behind her eyes. "StillFalling, whoever you are, if not for the grace of God we'd all stand before Him ashamed and condemned. I wore the labels alcoholic, bad friend, gossip, and sinner. But now, I wear the robes of righteousness bought by Christ's blood. He superimposes the reality that I was saved, am saved, and am being saved over the fact that I was an addict, am an addict, and will always be an addict. My addiction doesn't get to define me. He does."

StillFalling responded, *You've overcome a lot.*

"Jesus overcame a lot," she corrected.

You're an inspiration.

"Praise the Lord, this time I will inspire others for Him."

Are you changing things?

"Everything changed when I realized it didn't matter if I won or lost the Fan Favorite Choice Award. It didn't matter if no one picked me because God had chosen me, and because of that, I will never be alone."

Something that had been more important to her than anything else ceased to matter because the Lord mattered more. The weight of a million pounds lifted.

Approval no longer defined her.

"Yes, things are changing," Kathryn replied. "My media channels will remain active, but I'm no longer covering the daily news. I'm not jumping back into the grind to produce live clips. I'll pop in and out with pre-recorded videos to keep you updated on things like—" Kathryn gestured to Tiff to pan the bakery. "Ethan's shop reopening tomorrow! I'm so proud of his hard work." She trailed her fingers along the countertop. "I recorded some before and after videos and I'll post those at a later date." A much later date, because she was learning about the balance and boundaries she needed to keep in place to stay healthy.

"This is Kathryn Withers—" Kathryn swallowed. Wait—

Her mom's name popped up her feed. *We are so very proud of you.*

Everything stopped. Her parents were watching? And they were proud? After everything she put them through, they were proud? Kathryn's throat swelled. The pressure behind her eyes threatened to spill onto her cheeks.

You are brave, strong, and inspiring. We always believed in you.

Viewers were hearting her mom's comment faster than Kathryn could count. Her head fuzzed. Was it possible that the shame and denial she'd attributed to her parents was actually a reflection of her own guilt?

Tiff waved like a wild woman. She spun the camera

to face her. "Hey everybody, I'm Tiff, and before Kathryn signs off, Ethan has something to say."

Ethan stepped into the frame and dropped to a knee, holding out a tiny black box.

Kathryn gasped. The tears she'd been fighting fell. Her heart thumped wildly as Ethan opened the velvety lid. Inside, a delicate ring sparkled.

This wasn't happening. It couldn't be happening. Kathryn didn't know what to do or say. Shock had stolen her voice and her thoughts.

"Kathryn Withers, I wavered on whether I should do this privately or publicly. In the end, I decided to do this online because I want the whole world to know you have changed my life for the better. Ever since we first met at summer camp when we were kids"—his words were hoarse and laced with emotion—"you've been an amazing friend and confidante. I can't imagine living another day without you in my life."

Kathryn lifted her gaze from the ring to his eyes.

"I've known you were the one since we were eight years old, and we spent afternoons catching insects. You'd catch them, set them free, and mumble something about all God's creation deserving to live."

Kathryn laughed. During these past few joy-filled months, she rediscovered that simple eight-year-old who loved to dig in the dirt.

"We belong together," Ethan said.

Her mouth twitched. "Like pork 'n' beans?"

"Like Barbie 'n' Ken." His lips turned up.

"Like peanut butter and jelly." She swayed closer and arched a brow in a challenge.

He accepted. "Like break 'n' enter."

Was he remembering the night he broke into her house to retrieve his grandmother's recipe? That was the night they got back together. The night they filmed in her kitchen a Sycamore Sunrise episode that prompted his dad to reach out and begin mending the rift between them.

"Salt 'n' pepper."

"Coffee 'n' cream."

"Ah, guys," Tiff interrupted. "You have a few online comments to address."

Ethan took Kathryn's phone from her hand and laughed as he read them out loud. "Just ask her already. Kiss her." Ethan's voice caught. "Your parents gave their blessing and my dad says, you're a keeper, just like my mom."

Kathryn's heart felt full.

"One guy says if I don't ask, he will." Ethan looked up and caught her gaze. "I can't have that."

Ethan picked up her hand. Kathryn's breath caught. Her lungs expanded until she thought they might burst.

"Kathryn Withers, will you make me the happiest man on earth and be the cheese to my macaroni?"

She burst out laughing. The cheese wasn't destined to stand alone after all.

"I mean, will you be my wife?"

She nodded almost imperceptibly before finally managing to whisper, "Yes!"

Ethan rose to his feet and embraced her tightly amid swelling cries from their friends, who had gathered behind. Kathryn laid her head on the chest of the man she'd always loved. They fit together perfectly. Like love and marriage.

To Sweet Beginnings in Sycamore Hill

FREE: SERIES INTRODUCTION

SERIES INTRODUCTION

TO SWEET BEGINNINGS IN *Sycamore* HILL

A SHORT STORY SEQUENCE

STACEY WEEKS

Sign up for Stacey's newsletter and see how it all began for the couples you love from Sycamore Hill.

When a whistleblower speaks up, she tips the first domino of a twenty-four-hour chain reaction on the eve of Sycamore Hill's most important holiday event. A baker gets a career-making opportunity, a reporter chases the truth, a woman faces her greatest fear, and a lost child returns as the dominos continue to fall. The residents of Sycamore Hill approach a new year, and five couples celebrate sweet beginnings filled with endless possibilities in this short story sequence.

OWEN AND GLORIA: THURSDAY 2:00 P.M.

Sycamore Hill's prodigal daughter returns, shaking up the small town, righting a wrong, and finding the faith and family she'd lost along the way.

Gloria hasn't returned to Sycamore Hill since her university declared her guilty of cheating. She'd lost more than her home that day; she'd lost her faith in humanity. But when a questionable drug study with ties to the university endangers the residents of a Sycamore Hill ministry, Gloria can no longer remain quiet. She returns to town, and Owen—the town's unmarried pastor and the only person who believed in her innocence—helps her to finally and truly come home.

ETHAN AND KATHRYN: THURSDAY 11:59 P.M.

When you mix two former sweethearts, one missing recipe, and a dash of secrecy, what do you get? A recipe for romance!

Kathryn took something that belongs to Ethan. Correction. It belongs to his family. Taking it back isn't stealing, and letting himself into Kathryn's house to get it is not breaking and entering if he has a key. However, Kathryn's not a thief. She'd found Ethan's recipe. But when her actions threaten to spoil Ethan's bakery, they whip up a solution on Kathryn's internet morning show, Sycamore Hill at Sunrise.

BEN AND EMMA: FRIDAY 3:00 A.M.

God closes a door, but He opens a skylight, entwining Ben and Emma's future in the twilight hours of a winter's eve.

Nursing school made dating impossible for Emma, and now that she finally has time to think about a relationship, the pickings are slim, especially in a small town like Sycamore Hill. She's begun petitioning the Lord to drop Mr. Right into her life, ideally before a black-tie gala fundraiser. She can't bear the idea of attending alone —again.

When Ben—a local reporter—chases the scoop of a lifetime, he falls painfully into Emma's kitchen. With a whistleblower about to rip the lid off a scandal that'll put the small town on the map, Ben needs Emma's help to follow the career-making lead and protect the residents of Sycamore Hill.

ELI AND MEG: FRIDAY 7:35 A.M.

At some point, a girl has to stop running and fight.

Eli is willing to help Meg, but how can he fight an unknown enemy?

Eli and Meg trained together every morning to prepare for an annual road race. When Meg is uncharacteristically late on race day, Eli knows in his gut that something is wrong. He finds Meg facing her greatest fear, and Eli thrusts himself between her and an aggressive animal. However, when Meg passes up an opportunity to escape to safety, he realizes no one in Sycamore Hill really knows Meg at all.

JACKSON AND KIM: FRIDAY, 6:00 P.M. AND SATURDAY MORNING

Kim didn't want to like her ex's twin brother, but how could she not like the man returning her abducted son?

Kim doesn't have the mental headspace to host the black-tie gala on the eve of her abducted son's homecoming, but she must. As she grapples with conflicting emotions about the morning reunion, she clings to the message of Christmas: God with us.

Returning his nephew to Canada destroyed Jackson's relationship with his twin brother. And after all his brother had put Kim through, she might not welcome the continued presence of Jackson or his parents in Sycamore Hill. Sorting out the legalities won't be easy, but the right thing rarely is. Jackson will do what is right, whatever the personal cost, trusting the message of the season.

Sign up for Stacey's newsletter and read for free! If you're already subscribed, input the email you subscribed with and you'll be able to download the ebook.

The Sycamore Standoff
BOOK 1

Eli and Meg's story continues in The Sycamore Standoff, where Meg wants independence and Eli wants her affections. They'll have to face her past for any chance of a future.

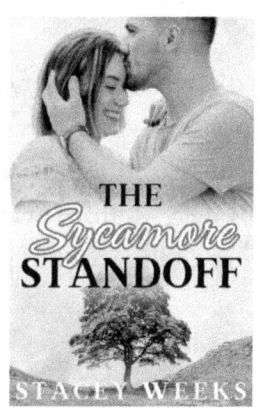

A man with a plan. A woman with a past. A thorny adventure called love.

Welcome to Sycamore Hill, where hearts mend, redemption is within reach, and love's blossoms endure even the harshest storms.

Landscape Architect Meg Gilmore's past resurfaces, threatening the harmony she's fought to cultivate. She's forced to confront the powerful family of Eli Martin, a friend she thought she could trust. With a 250-year-old tree—the very heart of Sycamore Hill—at stake, Meg and Eli's goals intertwine. For now.

Eli's roots run as deep as the ancient tree, and his noble intentions clash with familial expectations. He tries to help Meg—the first woman to see beyond his wealth and status—but only jeopardizes their future. Will Eli and Meg find their way out of the weeds and let love bloom, or will their secrets tear them apart?

Explore themes of trust, forgiveness, community, and the resilience of love in this stirring tale of redemption. Fans of Karen Kingsbury and Deborah Raney will love The Sycamore Standoff. Buy now before the price changes!

His Sycamore Sweetheart

BOOK 2

Follow Owen and Gloria's story in His Sycamore Sweetheart where Owen and Gloria navigate the messy (and sometimes hilarious) muddy water of dating in the public eye, where nothing is private, and everything is up for debate.

CHAPTER ONE - HIS SYCAMORE SWEETHEART

It could be worse.

Illuminated only by the light of the moon and several strategically-placed motion sensor lights, Gloria Sycamore fisted her hands on her hips. The toe of her three-inch-heeled boot tapped on the asphalt as she surveyed the jam-packed storage unit. Correction—overflowing storage unit. The contents of her life spilled out of the orange, garage-style door. Gloria righted a toaster tipped on its side, and her stomach lurched, just as it always did at the sight of her independence packed neatly into cardboard boxes with the top flaps folded over.

Just folded, not taped.

And neatly was a stretch.

A dot of sweat dribbled down her neck, between her shoulder blades, and over each bump in her spine in its descent. Her long-sleeved T-shirt stuck to her body like shrink wrap, and tendrils of frizzy, blonde hair had loosened from her ponytail, growing fatter and fatter with each passing, clammy second. The post-sunset coolness of the late September evening did little to moderate her inner, raging furnace. Acrylic fingernails one through eight dug into her palms and nine and ten lay somewhere on the ground underneath her sea of belongings. She stepped around the box erupting with scarves and shoes she'd never wear in a small town as far behind in fashion trends as Sycamore Hill. In three long strides, she reached the open trunk of her car, pivoted, and paced back.

The top half of the storage unit had lots of space, but Gloria didn't have the upper body strength to stack the boxes any higher. She should have waited for Owen. Correction. She had waited for Owen. She'd waited a whole hour. Sixty minutes. Three thousand, six hundred seconds. Now, ninety minutes later, she'd done the best she could, and it still wasn't good enough. It was the tagline of her life. All twenty-four years. Eight thousand, seven hundred and sixty-some-odd days of not being good enough. Her armpits dampened. She'd blame the growing stains on the physical labor. Not her perceived failure.

Owen was the one who'd picked a Wednesday night for her to move her belongings home. When Gloria announced that she'd given up her apartment in the city, Owen assured her parents that he'd help her, and there was no need for her dad to risk twinging his back again. Okay. Giving up her apartment was a stretch, too. Lost was a bit more accurate. Unable-to-pay-the-rent-when-she-didn't-have-a-job hit even closer to the truth. Evicted, if she was being totally honest. But this wasn't about her failure. It was about Owen's. He said that church meetings happened on Tuesday nights. Wednesday was clear. Wednesday was free. On Wednesday, he'd be all hers.

And in a nanosecond of terrible clarity, she understood what she'd been trying their entire relationship to not think about. Owen would never be wholly hers. Not as long as he was a pastor. He belonged to the church—the only acceptable mistress.

She puffed out a breath that failed to loosen the tension squeezing her chest. If Owen had come, he would have stacked the boxes. Then, she'd have a bit more room and all ten fingernails. But instead of enjoying Owen's dry banter and benefitting from his upper body strength, she paced in front of unit twenty-one, the one that spewed waves of stuff into view of anyone who happened to drive by the fenced-off self-storage business on the outskirts of town. She pressed her lips together. What to do, what to do.

The little piggy that went to market jammed against the edge of a box with the word *books* scrawled in black permanent marker on the side. As her toe painfully compressed, Gloria threw her hands out to the sides for balance and knocked over a coat rack. She hopped on one foot and shook out the other, her jerky movements knocking the flap of the closest box open because, of course, she didn't tape that one shut, either. The rhyme scheme from the familiar storybook sitting on top mocked her. *When life pours you lemons, think lemonade. When the sun gets too hot, be thankful for shade.*

She could use a cool drink of lemonade right about now. Her inability to secure a job after her co-op placement at Grander Nursery School ended had necessitated her move back home. Gloria didn't want to feel thankful things weren't worse, because right now, as she wondered who watched her from the vehicle that crawled down the road at a snail's pace, life felt pretty bad. Unfair. Rip-roaringly frustrating. Still, she automatically followed the directions she gave her precious kiddos. Find the good.

Worse would be not having a place to store her things while she temporarily moved back into her parents' home. Worse would be needing to live in her childhood home, when instead, she'd chosen to. Sure, the alternative was going into debt and living on credit, but it was still a choice—big difference. Worse would be losing eight more fingernails and adding a headache. Worse would be — She caught her reflection in a mirror leaning against the corner. Frizzy, blonde curls. Skin flushed to the point of blotchiness. Damp circles under her armpits. Worse would be Owen showing up and seeing her like this and deciding that maybe she wasn't the girl for him after all. *No matter how awful or ugly it gets, you can be thankful for something, I'd bet—*

"Need a hand?" Owen Mason's question interrupted the catchy rhyme.

Worse had found her again. And instead of offering her lemonade, she got to suck the juices from plain old, sour lemons. Her mouth puckered.

Despite just thinking—literally three seconds ago— that it was good Owen wasn't here, her body responded positively to his warm timbre. His words wrapped around her like a hug that she needed to shrug out of. She didn't turn around. She wasn't in a forgiving mood any more than she was in a thankful one.

"I know what you're thinking." She spoke to the wall.

"Do you?"

She heard his smile, and it sanded a tiny bit of the edge off her annoyance. She drummed her fingers on her hips. "You're probably thinking, 'How did such a young and successful woman like Gloria Sycamore end up back in Sycamore Hill, living with her parents?'"

He chuckled. It started low and rumbled like the trolley carts the storage unit provided customers for hauling stuff from the trunk of their cars to the units. Carts she wouldn't have used had Owen shown up on time. The heat building in her chest cooled a bit. His footsteps dragged along the pavement with a scuffing sound. She could feel him moving closer. It had always been that way with them.

"What else am I thinking?" His quiet question caressed the back of her neck, and she shivered from the warmth of his breath. She tried to hang onto her frustration, but she couldn't stay mad at him. She never could. She leaned into him and further into their game.

"You're wondering if the only reason she came back is because she couldn't get a job."

"Try again."

"You're wondering if she came back because her family lives here."

"Wrong." He loosely wrapped his arms around her middle and tugged her until her back pressed against his chest. If her sweaty dampness bothered him, he didn't show it.

"You're wondering if she is ready for all the changes coming her way."

He dropped a kiss on her temple.

"Because she's thinking those things," Gloria muttered.

"Are those the only reasons she came back?"

This time, steamy warmth tickled her earlobe, deliciously toasting her insides like marshmallows over a campfire. Gloria melted like s'mores. "You're wondering if any other reason drew her back to Sycamore Hill."

"I am." He cinched his arms tighter and rested his chin on the top of her head. They fit perfectly like that. She stood one head shorter, even with heels. She always felt safe tucked into his arms.

"Maybe," she murmured, not voicing the remaining questions that flitted through her mind.

He's wondering if she's pastor-wife material.

He's wondering if his congregation will accept her.

He's wondering if she'll find a new job in Sycamore Hill and stay for good.

He's wondering if they have a future.

He's wondering if she's wondering about those things.

Because she was.

Gloria twisted into Owen's arms and rested her cheek against his chest. The solid throbbing of his heart steadied her. Sure, it was simpler when she lived in the city, but long distance only worked for so long. Still, no one in the city cared who Pastor Owen of Sycamore Hill Community Church dated. Everyone in Sycamore Hill cared. They not only cared, but they held strong opinions. Strong enough that, up until this point, Owen set most of their dates in the city. He came to her. He insisted.

Was that because he shared her unspoken questions?

She inhaled his spicy aftershave until her lungs felt like they'd burst. She briefly held onto his scent before slowly letting the air escape between her tight lips. Regardless of what anyone else thought about her return to Sycamore Hill or her growing romance with Owen, Gloria was home. For better or worse. Gloria had to get some distance from the controversial trial and the hounding journalists that dubbed her *Gloria the whistleblower*. She'd exposed a falsified drug trial nine months ago. Now that her name had been cleared—finally—she could come home and hold her head high. The only questions that remained were how the courts would punish her former classmate and roommate for her deception and whether the big company, Emergence Pharmaceuticals, would survive the scandal.

"You're trembling." Owen rubbed his hands up and down her back, adding a delightful friction to her stirred-up insides. "Are you okay?"

"Just tired." Tired of interviews. Tired of depositions. Tired of testifying. Tired of her hero-move mucking up her life. All she ever wanted was a peaceful, quiet existence. But leaving university under headlines that accused her of cheating, starting and finishing her education after a career change to Early Childhood Education, testifying in court, and now dating the well-loved, small-town pastor was anything but peaceful and quiet.

But that was a fight for another day.

Another forceful exhalation lifted most of Gloria's bangs off her forehead. A few sweaty strands stuck like glue. Gloria's parents had raised her to do the right thing no matter what it cost. And despite being the black sheep of her over-achieving family, that lesson stuck. Better to complicate her life than let the residents of Life House, the vulnerable clients on which Emergence had slated to begin human drug trials, suffer. The women trying to rebuild their life deserved better. Her gaze found the nursery rhyme book cover again.

The rain hits the dirt, and the dirt turns to mud, and it slips, and it slides, and it spreads like a flood.

Her involvement with the case did bring her together with Owen again, spreading a little sugar on the oozy-doozy mud pie that was her life. She lifted her face to his.

But Owen's gaze wasn't on her. It was tripping over the twenty or so boxes still looking for a spot in her unit. "I thought I told you to wait for me, and I would help you unload?" There was only the tiniest amount of admonishment in Owen's tone, but it was enough to annoy like a fingernail on a chalkboard.

Two broken fingernails, to be more precise.

"I thought you'd be here at seven o'clock."

He chuckled again. Was everything funny to him? "I had a small church emergency. One of the deacons called as I was heading out the door."

The church. By tomorrow, the church would know she was back, and someone was bound to speculate on what it meant for her, Owen, and the congregation. If Gloria's friends were right, the people would pull out their scorecards and begin tracking tally marks. Was she worthy of their pastor's affections? Was quitting the sciences and trading beakers and test tubes for preschool rhymes an acceptable decision? They'd rank her reliability as a witness in the biggest scandal to impact the town, score her clothing choices, and decide on her overall suitability as a small-town ministry wife. Tonight, the match was tied at zero, but tomorrow? That was anyone's game.

Oozy-doozy, indeed.

Gloria pulled out of Owen's arms. Coolness hit her sweaty skin, and her flesh prickled. She yanked a sweater out of a nearby box, snagging the cuff and pulling loose a thread. Great. Just great. Was this her future if things worked out for them? Her waiting for him, him prioritizing the church, her making do on her own, sacrificing fingernails, mental health, and her favorite sweater? Was his delay the result of a preemptive strike from Sycamore Hill Community Church? Were they letting her know where she ranked on the scale of priorities? If they were, it was mighty passive-aggressive of them. But passive-aggressive was the weapon of choice for most church-goers.

She lifted her shoulder in a shrug as if it was no big deal. Really, she couldn't complain about the church needing him without sounding like a whiny baby. "I managed."

"Did you?" Owen cocked an eyebrow. He twisted his lips to the right, strolled over to the largest box, labeled off-season clothes, and peeked inside. "You have a lot of stuff."

I've not seen a mess that I cannot wrangle, 'till I met this web that I cannot untangle!

There was no way to know if the quirky rhyme applied more to her storage unit or life. "Was it anything serious with the church emergency?" She lobbed out a lame question. A filler. A way to deflect from the things they should have been talking about.

"Only if you call a leaky roof serious, but Jason had to go through it point by point right then. It couldn't wait." Owen made the kind of noise that told Gloria being a pastor wasn't all sunshine and roses. Her compassion spiked a notch until she did the math.

The things that ranked higher in importance than her were phone calls from the deacons, a leaky roof, church business, and some annoyed guy named Jason. Good to know. Her gaze found her book again.

Be true to what's you, be you all the way. They can't take from you what you won't give away.

Maybe.

169

Maybe not.

*Read the rest of Owen and Gloria's story in His Sycamore Sweetheart.

Gloria Sycamore returns to Sycamore Hill and takes on the ultimate challenge: regaining the town's trust while juggling the hilarious and downright chaotic pleasure of dating their beloved minister. Under the watchful eyes of the public, privacy is a luxury, and every decision she makes is open for debate.

Pastor Owen finds himself stuck between a rock and a hard pew when rumors of biblical proportions create a divine dilemma for him and Gloria. The congregation's collective eyebrows shoot higher than the church steeple as whispers reverberate through the hallowed halls. Owen struggles to balance his flock's demands with his heart's desires. Will he rise to the occasion, or will he find himself delivering sermons to an empty room?

Despite Gloria's illustrious family name and Owen's honourable character, Gloria and Owen are caught in the throes of a scandal. As the community continues to question Gloria's commitment to her faith, the town, and their treasured pastor, the pews become a battleground for an uproarious holy war.

Hold on to your pew, don your finest church hat, and prepare for a side-splitting journey of misadventure in this delightful blend of faith and devotion topped with a whole lot of heart. A captivating romance, witty narrative, and a quirky collection of unforgettable characters guarantee His Sycamore Sweetheart will have you cheering for Gloria and Owen as they fumble their way to true love.

Order now!

The Sycamore Slopes

BOOK 3

Follow Ben and Emma's story in The Sycamore Slopes as they try to unite the split town before an avalanche of trouble buries them.

When a family is torn apart, the battle lines are drawn and the fight to control Sycamore Hill heats up.

Ben Sawyer gives the vulnerable a voice and strives to protect them, but he can't stop the avalanche of trouble descending on his nephew. His strongest opponent isn't the grumpy Grinch sowing discord in the community, but the one person he believed would always be by his side: Nurse Practitioner Emma Powles.

Emma Powles is busy in her newly established medical clinic as the fallout from sledding and skating accidents inundates the clinic. She treats the suspicious injuries of a local child and she's forced to intervene for the girl's safety. Her actions rouse traumatic memories in Ben, testing the foundation of their relationship. Will the echoes of Ben's past shatter their future?

The Sycamore Slopes is an enthralling romance that seamlessly weaves together family drama, small-town politics, and powerful themes of resilience.

Order now!

One Sycamore
Sunday

BOOK 4

Follow Jackson and Kim's story in One Sycamore Sunday. Kim's day begins like any other until one terrifying moment changes everything.

It started as a normal Sunday, but one horrifying moment changed everything forever.

When a group of men abduct her son, Kim Jansen turns

to the only person she can trust—Jackson McGregor. Officer McGregor would trade his life for the boy, but it's not McGregor the kidnappers want. They want a woman Kim helped disappear, and they've taken Kim's son as leverage. As McGregor races to save the boy, Kim faces an impossible choice—protect her friend or save her child.

One Sycamore Sunday is a high-stakes, fast-paced romance.

Order now!

Acknowledgments

Writing is never a one-person adventure. Despite the hours I live inside my head working on a story, countless others invest in the project. Sycamore Hill exists because my friends in the Brantford Writers Group believed in it. Thank you.

A special thanks to Rick Ryerse for your policing expertise and to Elio J Caporicci from Early Bird Coffee for taking me on my first roasting tour and answering my endless questions about all the ways I could sabotage Ethan's coffee roasting adventure. All mistakes are mine.

A final thank you to an extraordinary editor, Olivia, from LivEdits. You helped tie the threads of this story and series together beautifully. Your little notes of "wow" or "loved this" cheered me on the hard days. You are a blessing.

About the Author

Stacey is a ministry wife, mother of three teenagers, and a sipper of hot tea with honey. She loves to open the Word of God and share the hope of Christ with women. She is a multi-award-winning author, the primary home-educator of her children, and a frequent conference speaker. Stacey has a Graduate Certificate in Women's Ministry from Heritage College and Seminary and a Graduate Certificate in Biblical Counselling.

f facebook.com/writerSWeeks

X x.com/writerSWeeks

⬡ instagram.com/writersweeks

You Can Make a Difference

Did you enjoy this book? You can make a difference. Honest reviews of books bring them to the attention of other readers. If you enjoyed this book, I would be grateful if you could spend a few minutes to leave an online review.

- Goodreads

www.ingramcontent.com/pod-product-compliance
Lightning Source LLC
Chambersburg PA
CBHW060441180626
46817CB00007B/2918